Matthew o...
maedel was being threatened...

As she darted her gaze around the bus terminal, perhaps looking for an escape, Matthew waved his hand low to get her attention.

She stared directly at him, and he could see she had startling green eyes. He slowly tilted his head toward the door he held open. She paused and stared at the van, seeming to evaluate her options and make a decision.

The green-eyed *maedel* barreled toward him and the minivan, before whispering a "thanks" and stepping inside the well at the back of the van.

"Ready, Matthew?" Mr. Jones called from the driver's seat.

But he hadn't moved fast enough.

"Hey!" The assailant with the gun started toward him from the terminal door, malice emanating from her pinched eyebrows and clenched fists, the gun now aimed at him. A man had joined her. "Stop! I see her in there!"

"Let's go," Matthew hollered.

But as he rounded the back of the van in haste to get to his seat, a gunshot exploded in the terminal...

By sixth grade, **Meghan Carver** knew she wanted to write. After a degree in English from Millikin University, she detoured to law school, completing a Juris Doctor from Indiana University. She then worked in immigration law and taught college-level composition. Now she homeschools her six children with her husband. When she isn't writing, homeschooling or planning the family's next travel adventure, she is active in her church, sews for her kidlets and reads.

Books by Meghan Carver

Love Inspired Suspense

Under Duress
Deadly Disclosure
Amish Country Amnesia
Amish Covert Operation

Plain Secrets

Amish Country Hideout

Visit the Author Profile page at LoveInspired.com.

AMISH COUNTRY HIDEOUT

MEGHAN CARVER

LOVE INSPIRED SUSPENSE
INSPIRATIONAL ROMANCE

MIX
Paper | Supporting
responsible forestry
FSC® C021394

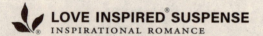

LOVE INSPIRED® SUSPENSE
INSPIRATIONAL ROMANCE

Recycling programs
for this product may
not exist in your area.

ISBN-13: 978-1-335-95759-7

Amish Country Hideout

Love Inspired
22 Adelaide St. West, 41st Floor
Toronto, Ontario M5H 4E3, Canada
www.LoveInspired.com

HarperCollins Publishers
Macken House, 39/40 Mayor Street Upper,
Dublin 1, D01 C9W8, Ireland
www.HarperCollins.com

Printed in Lithuania

If the Son therefore shall make you free,
ye shall be free indeed.
—*John* 8:36

To my family, my biggest encouragers and most ardent supporters. I love doing life with you!

ONE

Veronica Williams felt like she had been holding her breath for over a decade as she scanned the parking lot visible through her living room window. She couldn't see anything unusual out there, despite what she had heard on the police-scanner app about a prisoner escape from the women's jail. She remained safe, at least for this moment. That penitentiary was located several states away. Constant surveillance was second nature now, she realized, as she dumped the chicken-flavored powder into the water-and-noodle mixture, swished a spoon around the large mug and popped the dish into the microwave.

The machine groaned, and she thunked it on the top until it stopped. It was probably time to splurge for a new one, but she dreaded leaving the apartment to go shopping. Although twenty years had passed since she had sworn to tell the truth, the whole truth and nothing but the truth to put a child trafficker behind bars, her heart would still climb into her throat at the question of who might be on the other side of her door.

Chicken-flavored noodles were not exactly the gourmet meal some might expect from the successful cookbook author and web chef who went by the nom de plume Penelope Cupcake, but tonight she just didn't feel like cooking. She was human, too, and sometimes she needed an afternoon of convenience food and a long novel to escape the real world.

She counted down the last ten seconds as the spicy chicken scent began to waft through her tiny living area, her stomach growling at the aroma.

A harsh voice was being broadcast from the scanner app on her phone, where it rested on the side table across the room. More news, but this time it was local. An insistent, grating ring of panic tolled in her ears. In a discordant stridency, it soon harmonized with the dinging of the microwave. Oblivious now to her lunch, Veronica stared at her phone, concentrating on the report of suspicious activity in her area. A pizza delivery kid had had his pizzas stolen.

Dread climbed up her spine and settled at the back of her neck. Her brain told her it was irrational to panic over a stolen pizza, but her heart still thumped erratically at the what-ifs.

After two decades of hiding, she felt truly threatened. A woman had escaped from the prison where the child trafficker had been incarcerated, and a delivery boy in town had his goods stolen. She couldn't explain it, but the goose bumps on her arms told her those two events were related. Had her identity been compromised? And then, something clicked in her mind. On instinct, a list of items to take and a sequence of events to follow that she hadn't thought through in years was resurrected, and she sprang into action.

With a deep breath, she snatched her driver's license from the table. In a glance, she scanned the address printed there, a place she would probably never call home again. There wasn't time for nostalgia or wishful thinking. Her social security card was next, the one that finally looked its age, even though it was less than half her natural years. She ran a hand quickly through her hair. At the tender age of ten, she had endured things that no girl should have to suffer, and now, it seemed that prior life had caught up with her.

Department-store hide-and-seek in the clothing racks had been Veronica's favorite childhood game whenever her parents shopped.

Until that particular day.

As she and her two younger sisters had peeked out of their hiding spot, a dark-haired woman wearing a colorful scarf had snatched a toddler from a shopping cart as the mother focused intently on the shelf of merchandise. Distracted by a new toy the woman offered, the child barely made a sound as the woman handed her off to a man waiting in the next aisle who'd had his back to the sisters. When the woman had attempted to snatch another youngster from a different cart, Veronica's parents noticed and protested, only to be gunned down by the woman. With the testimony of the three sisters, the woman had been convicted, but law enforcement never discovered the man's identity. The danger of the unknown accomplice seeking retribution against them landed the girls in the witness protection program—they were separated to different arrangements and never saw each other again.

It had been no fault of her own. Life in WITSEC had been thrust upon her when she'd had had no choice but to comply. Hiding had been her only option, or she would never have survived. For twenty years, she had persevered and done her level best to adjust to a new name and place, a new background. A new *her*. Yet it seemed it hadn't been enough.

Whatever had happened with those child traffickers, she was, apparently, in danger again.

Now, at the age of thirty, she grabbed the last of her

documents and headed to the closet. From the bottom, she retrieved her go bag, something she had kept prepared for the bulk of her time spent hiding. She quickly thumbed through the contents, searching her memory for the last time she had switched out the protein bars and bottles of water for fresh items. It didn't matter. There wasn't time. What she had would have to suffice. At the bottom, she found her passport with the name *Veronica Williams*, a couple of photos she had managed to save from her childhood that not even her handler with the US Marshal's office knew she had in her possession and a yellowed map of the current area where she lived.

In her haste, she slid across the kitchen floor, grabbed her purse and stuffed it down in the go bag. She jerked open the freezer door and ripped out an envelope that was taped to the side of the inside wall. That stash of cash would be invaluable wherever she ended up.

She pushed the freezer closed as a loud knock sounded on her apartment door. Startled, she dropped the envelope, then fell quickly to the floor to retrieve several twenty-dollar bills that had slid out. Hunkered down, she froze, immobilized as if that would prevent her detection by whomever was at the door. She knew almost no one and rarely had anything delivered. That knock could only mean one thing.

Trouble.

The knock sounded again, this time louder. More insistent. She stood slowly and tucked the envelope of cash deep inside the bag, then dropped it to the floor. Thankful that she had on her quietest shoes, she crept to the door and stood for a moment, listening for movement on the other side.

Veronica rose up to peer through the peephole. Twenty years ago, the gang had operated as if they were professionals. There was no reason to think they would have lost any skill in remaining undetected. A pizza delivery guy stood there, staring directly at the peephole. His stare was focused and intense, not the slack-jawed boredom of someone who didn't want to do a tedious job.

She sucked in her breath and stepped back from the door, her hand rising to fist the front of her blouse. Pizza? She hadn't ordered anything. And after all these years of hiding, she knew absolutely no one who would be so kind as to buy a pizza and have it sent to her house. Was her isolation why this man was so bold as to approach in the middle of the afternoon and not wait for the cover of darkness? Her blood suddenly felt icy in her veins, and she rubbed at the goose bumps on her arms.

Moving to peer through the hole one more time, she held her breath and then crept back to retrieve her bag from the kitchen floor. It was time to leave.

Quietly, she crossed to a window and lifted it. After climbing over the sill, she stood on the fire escape and closed the window. With one last quick survey of the inside of the apartment she had called home for several years, she turned her back on the life she had meticulously built and curated out of nothing.

She shimmied down the rusty metal of the ladder, refusing to look down the three flights to the ground. Hunched over to stay out of sight, she made her way across the parking lot to her car. She shouldn't drive it. There was no way she could tell if it had been tampered with, but a classic attack strategy would be to cut the line to the brakes or attach a bomb that would blow when she turned the ignition. Veronica sighed. It had been a good vehicle, and she touched the hood as a goodbye as she hurried past. At the corner of the lot, she unlocked her bicycle from the rack, glancing up at her window as she pulled it from between the rungs.

The delivery guy stood at her window, a weapon of some sort in his hand and not the pizza box. For a moment, her eyes caught his, her heart pressing against her rib cage. She swiped her hands on her shirt to dry the perspiration on her palms and grabbed the handlebars of her bicycle. With her go bag slung across her body, she mounted the bike and pushed hard on the pedals to propel herself around the corner. Once out of sight of the man in her apartment who no doubt had malicious intent, she breathed deeply. Maybe that fresh air would jump-start her courage.

Whoever that man was, he was not the one she had sent to prison with her testimony. Maybe he was the woman's partner in crime, the guy in the department store who had had his back turned to her and her sisters. The woman's name flooded back with a tsunami of memories—Nadia Popov. Of course, she would have associates, and that meant that Veronica needed to be extra cautious as she made her escape.

Over the years, Veronica had traveled the back alleys and side roads of Fort Wayne, a medium-size city in northern Indiana, learning and memorizing everything in preparation for such a moment as this. She cut down an alley in between two residential buildings, heading in the general direction of the bus station downtown, and then crossed another parking lot to an alley that ran behind a retail center. A glance over her shoulder revealed nothing, but there she had a sense the perpetrator was close behind. She pedaled past the back entrance of an Italian restaurant that was popular with the people who worked in nearby offices. The lunch crowd would just now be thinning out as employees headed back to their desks, and the aroma of garlic and sauce nearly knocked her off her bicycle. Her stomach growled in protest as she rushed past.

She turned a corner just a few blocks from the bus station, swerving around a dumpster as she glanced back over her shoulder again.

It was amazing, yet also shocking with a hint of dismay, how quickly her instincts had returned. The same habits and practices from twenty years ago had been resurrected almost instantly. The deputy marshal had promised safety and security, as long as she followed his rules. But she had decided back then that she needed to be responsible for *herself*. Never again would she place her life in someone else's hands. Her parents weren't there anymore. Her two sisters had been forced to go their separate ways. She had known, even as a ten-year-old, that eventually, the deputy marshal would go on to another witness and she would be the only one left to watch her own back.

No, there was no one she could trust.

The tears hit hard and fast. In a few seconds, they were cascading down her cheeks and blurring her vision. Her chest heaved as she let out great sobs, but she forced herself to continue pedaling. Veronica inhaled deeply once again. She was losing her presence of mind, helpless to stop the flow, and the long breath of oxygen only caused hiccups.

She had wondered about this day, *this moment*, many times. Thought she would be better at leaving her life behind this time since she'd done it before when she entered WITSEC. But she'd let herself feel relatively safe in her town, in her apartment. She'd settled in. And now, she was uprooting all over again. A thousand doubts pricked her mind as what seemed like a thousand tears distorted her vision. Had she grabbed her photo album? Did she have more to eat than the protein bars in her bag? Had she destroyed the bills on the desk that had her new name on them? No, no and no.

Veronica swerved around a corner, and the bus station loomed up in front of her. She drove her bicycle into the rack and dismounted, swiping at the moisture on her cheeks and snuffling up any tears that continued to threaten to flow. Not wanting to draw any attention to herself. Then she dropped the kickstand but didn't bother to lock up the bike. She wouldn't be back for it.

Inside the terminal, she found a quiet corner and reached into the pocket of the bag where her phone should be. Nothing. She sagged against the wall. What was wrong with her? She finally had a moment to telephone the number she had memorized two decades ago, but she had taken off without retrieving her cell phone from the charging station. The grouchy-looking ticket agent had a sign indicating that he had no phone available, and there was no one else around with a phone to borrow. Pay phones had gone the way of the dinosaurs, so she had no way to contact the US Marshals office.

Squaring her shoulders, she crossed to the ticket counter. It didn't matter where the bus was going, she would get on whichever one left next. The grimy floor was in need of a good scrubbing, and the trash can near the door was overflowing. But she'd been in worse bus stations, especially in those early days on the run. In those first few months, hiding and being shuffled from place to place as she waited for the trial, when the fear of an accomplice coming after her was very real, she had seen plenty of unseemly places. Still, the odors of motor oil and perspiration assaulted her, and a wish to be back at the Italian restaurant flitted through her consciousness.

The arrivals-and-departures board showed that a bus

headed to Indianapolis had pulled out just three minutes ago. She must have had a look of frustration or disappointment on her face, for the lone ticket agent, an older man with a balding forehead, leaned across the counter. "Miss, what are you looking for?"

"Um…" Should she just admit that she would go anywhere? She didn't want to raise any red flags, but she also had to get on a bus as soon as possible.

An irritated grimace dimpled the man's face. "The next bus leaves in an hour, headed to St. Louis." He nodded toward the tall windows that looked out on a bus that was beginning to unload passengers. "That one."

An hour? What would she do until then? But with no other options, she stepped to the counter and dug out the cash for the ticket. At least St. Louis would be two states away. "Thank you." She fought hard to keep her voice from wobbling.

After stashing the ticket in a pocket of her bag, she turned from the counter. A woman stood in the doorway, with dark hair and even darker eyes, and a brightly colored scarf around her neck. A gasp escaped unbidden, and Veronica sidestepped slowly toward the door that led to the loading area. Was that the same woman, the cold-blooded killer she had faced in the courtroom all those years ago? She couldn't be sure since it had been so long and Veronica had only been ten years old then. But the woman looked enough like her that desperation to disappear from sight rose up in her chest.

Once through the doors and out in the loading bay, Veronica drifted toward a couple of vending machines, forcing herself to look as nonchalant as possible. Through the large windows that allowed him to keep an eye on buses coming and going, the ticket agent gave her a quizzical look but then returned his attention to his computer. Where could she hide?

The vending machines looked ancient. Most likely, they hadn't been filled in years. But there was just enough space in between the two that she could insert herself into the tiny slot. She pulled in her bag after her just as the woman pushed through the terminal door. Even from a distance, Veronica could see the venomous sneer that snaked across the woman's face. Slowly, she pulled a gun from her voluminous handbag and pointed it at Veronica where she was stuck between the machines.

Had her past finally caught up with her?

Matthew Yoder grabbed his *schwester* Esther's suitcase and placed it on the asphalt next to her. The bus station was not a busy place in the middle of a Thursday, and for that, he was glad. Still, though, he would be even happier to get back home to their little community of Bent Grass in northern Indiana.

"Denki, mein bruder." The petite blond woman in front of him bore a striking resemblance to their *mamm*, a fact that alternately brought him either comfort or sorrow. A pang clenched his heart. Today, it was sorrow. "Are you alright?" she asked.

"Jah, just missing *Mamm* and *Daed."* He swung back to the pile of suitcases outside the bus and retrieved his own, then placed it next to his *schwester*'s.

"It is particularly difficult after visiting *Aendi* and *Oncle, jah*? They remind me so much of the *gut* times we used to have."

Matthew removed his hat and ran his hand through his hair, then returned the straw hat to his head. "It is *gut* but also painful to visit them in Lancaster County."

Esther stepped forward and laid her hand on his fore-arm. "Matthew, you are not to blame for the death of our parents. You did all you could, probably even more than you should have considering the danger of a *haus* on fire."

He looked down at his legs, one still a wee bit shorter than the other despite the shoe with the corrective heel. Normal was not something he would ever be again. "*Jah*, you have said that perhaps seven hundred times in the last ten years."

"And I will say it seven hundred more times if need be, *mein bruder*." A warm smile lit her face.

"'No one is useless in this world who lightens the burdens of another.' That is the wisdom of Charles Dickens." He forced himself to return her smile.

"I think you read every book you stock in that book-store of yours."

A blue minivan pulled into a space in the loading bay. "The taxi is here." Matthew nodded toward the vehicle as a slender woman who had squeezed herself in between two vending machines caught his eye. A look of fright flashed across her face as she briefly met his gaze.

He hefted both suitcases as Esther looped her bag across her front. His laborious gait had only taken him a few steps toward the Amish taxi when the woman in between the vending machines widened her eyes at him, her look of fear intensifying.

Was something going on at the bus station? It seemed that the *maedel* believed she was in danger. But from what? Or whom?

He halted and lowered the suitcases to the ground, noting that they were just a few yards from the machines. Perhaps it would be helpful to have the vehicle nearby. "Esther, I do not want to be a burden. But could you ask Mr. Jones to drive his van closer?"

"*Ach*, are you in pain?" She gave him a worried look.

"*Nee*, just ask him. Please."

Esther hurried away, and a few moments later, the minivan stopped right next to him. The driver bounded out and around to Matthew.

"*Gut* afternoon, Mr. Jones. *Denki* for coming for us." Matthew shook the driver's hand.

"Son, I've told you time and again to call me Amos." He opened the front passenger door for Esther to step into the seat.

"I know, Mr. Jones, but *mein mamm* taught me to treat *mein* elders and those in authority with respect. Calling you by your first name just does not seem respectful, and I cannot dishonor the memory of *mein mamm* that way."

"Fine. Fine. I understand. Your mother was a good Christian woman, and I wouldn't want you to feel like you weren't respecting her." Mr. Jones grabbed Esther's suitcase and loaded it into the back of his minivan.

Matthew looked back to the woman between the vending machines. She seemed to have squeezed herself farther into the shadows, and was clutching a navy blue bag as if it was her only lifeline. What frightened her? He looked around for the source of her panic. It was strangely empty, as a maintenance worker finished emptying a trash can and disappeared into a utility room. In the doorway between the terminal and the loading area, though, a woman with dark eyes stared intently at the vending machines. She held a gun, half-hidden by her large purse and pointed at the young woman.

As the woman slowly advanced on the machines, a protective instinct welled up from deep within him, the hair on the back of his neck standing at attention. He clenched his hands into fists.

Mr. Jones grabbed his suitcase and put it in the back of the van. "That's it. We're ready."

Matthew nodded, barely registering what the taxi driver had said. He stared at both women, trying to assess the situation. It would be easier just to let the frightened *maedel* between the vending machines be, since she was plainly an *Englischer* and had her own problems that had nothing to do with him. The Amish practice was to stay away from any sort of violence, and clearly, this dark-haired woman intended to inflict harm. But it was only a week or so ago that he had pulled out the big family Bible for the after-supper devotional and prayer and read aloud the story of the Good Samaritan. Matthew Yoder refused to be like the priest or the Levite and cross to the other side of the road when someone undoubtedly needed help. Anyone could see that the young *maedel*'s life was being threatened.

He glanced back at Mr. Jones. He had loaded all the luggage, closed the back doors and was waiting behind the wheel. Esther, in the passenger seat, had just turned to call to him to get going. Neither had noticed the dangerous standoff.

Keeping an eye on the malicious-minded woman, Matthew stepped backward to open the rear of the minivan again. As the *maedel* darted her gaze around the bus terminal, perhaps looking for an escape, he waved his hand low to get her attention.

She stared directly at him, and he could see she had startling green eyes. He slowly tilted his head toward the back of the van, simultaneously cutting his eyes toward the door he held open. She paused and stared at the van, the moments stretching into eternity as she seemed to evaluate her options and make a split-second decision.

Raucous laughter rose up from inside the terminal, drawing the attention of the woman with the gun for a moment. Matthew was also distracted and followed the line of sight through the windows. When he looked back to the space between the machines, the green-eyed *maedel* was barreling toward him and the minivan.

With great haste, he removed his smaller suitcase, holding it in front of himself as if it was a shield. The woman, with perspiration beaded on her brow and reddish-blond hair flying behind her, whispered a thank-you and stepped inside the well at the back of the van. He glanced around the loading area but couldn't quite tell if the older woman had seen where the younger woman had gone. She trained her gaze on him, making his heart pound as he spied the gun still in her hand. But he turned his back to her and placed his suitcase in the well directly in front of the stowaway. He had no idea where all that courage had come from, but he thanked *Gott* he could be helpful.

A throat clearing sounded from the front of the van, and Matthew looked up to see Esther questioning him with raised eyebrows. He shook his head slightly, hoping to indicate that she should not say anything. She seemed to understand as she turned to face the driver.

"Ready, Matthew?" Mr. Jones called from the driver's seat.

But he hadn't moved fast enough.

"Hey!" The dark-eyed woman started toward him from the terminal door, malice emanating from her pinched eyebrows and clenched fists, the gun now aimed at him. A man had joined her. "*Stop!* I see her in there!"

A chill wracked him at the icy evil present in her eyes and hardened on her face.

His heart leaped into his throat as he spun to stare down at the woman now hiding among the luggage. With a hard swallow, Matthew broke eye contact and stepped away. He slammed the back door shut then banged on it. "Let's go," he hollered to Mr. Jones.

But as he rounded the back of the van in haste to get to his seat, a gunshot exploded in the terminal. Everything blurred around him as he fell to the asphalt, his hands smacking the ground.

TWO

Footsteps pounded behind Matthew as he stared at the asphalt, blaming his disability. A *maedel*'s life may be in his hands, and he was lying helpless on the ground. He paused for a nanosecond to check himself for injuries, but nothing felt out of the ordinary. No pain. No stickiness of blood. He'd read that gunshots that grazed the skin created a stinging sensation, but he didn't have that, either. Pushing aside his shock, his mind rebelled at the fact that the woman had actually fired her weapon. What evil person would do that with the intent to harm or kill another?

Adrenaline continued to pulsate through his body, and he pushed himself up. He had an obligation to protect human life, and that was what he was going to do.

Without looking back, he rose to his feet, his knees shaking. Esther stared at him, her typical anxiety for his well-being etched into her features. She glanced behind him, and the hair on the back of Matthew's neck rose at the thought of how close their stowaway's pursuers might be. Pulling his lame leg forward, he treaded as quickly as he could to the side door of the minivan and slid into his seat. He slammed the door shut behind him.

Esther spun to face him. "What is happening? Are you alright?"

Grimacing from the discomfort in his leg, he simply nodded, then looked to Mr. Jones. "*Goh*. Quickly, please."

Still not turning around, Matthew allowed himself to sit back a little in his seat when the taxi driver took off without question. Esther's expression morphed from anxiety to a startled look of confusion. Riding in an automobile felt foreign enough, but in an escape like this? No wonder she was alarmed. Still, there needed to be nothing suspicious about them.

"Esther, *mein schwester*," he instructed her, keeping his voice low even as his heart threatened to pound out of his chest, "face forward. Look normal."

Mr. Jones quickly steered out of the bus station loading area. As the driver turned the van into the parking lot and headed toward the exit, Matthew allowed himself to look back. The man and woman ran close behind, but at the parking area, they veered away from the chase as if headed toward a vehicle. The Amish taxi pulled out of the lot and drove down the street and out of view of the bus terminal before he could identify their vehicle. He had no idea what kind of car they drove.

Matthew leaned forward and clapped the driver on the shoulder. "*Denki*, Mr. Jones. I apologize for the problem I may have caused. Rather than take this road straight home to Bent Grass, could you wind a little through the country? As a precaution." Whoever those two were, Matthew didn't trust their intentions, and he definitely did not want them to catch up with the Amish taxi.

Several miles of silence passed before Esther asked, "What is going on, Matthew?" She remained facing forward, but he could not mistake the tremble in her voice.

"It will be alright. I have helped someone in distress, and the best thing you can do right now is pray for *Gott*'s protection." He turned slightly to project his voice to the *maedel* hiding in the back with the luggage. "We have left the bus station, and I believe you are safe now. But I would caution you to stay down. Just in case."

Esther turned to shoot a quizzical look at him. In the rearview mirror, Matthew could see that Mr. Jones was confused as well, as he glanced quickly between the road and Matthew in the mirror, his graying eyebrows pulled down.

"Mein bruder." The trembling had left Esther's voice, and she sounded more firm. "What is going on?"

"We have an extra passenger. And Mr. Jones, I will gladly pay you for the trouble."

Esther shot her gaze around the small minivan, a hand on her starched white *kapp*. *"Ach*, what do you mean 'extra passenger'? Where?"

Matthew nodded toward the back. "I have let a *maedel* stow away with our luggage. An *Englischer*. She looked like she needed help. Is it not our Christian obligation to help those in need?" Would his sister understand? Would Mr. Jones? Though their driver was not of the Amish faith, he was a good man. But did it truly matter whether they accepted it or not? Matthew had done what his faith required of him.

From deep in the luggage, a quiet voice warbled, "Thank you."

"Are you hurt? Do you have enough room?"

"I wouldn't mind stretching my legs, but I'm fine for now." She paused. "Thank you again. I think you saved my life."

Matthew exchanged a look of raised eyebrows with Esther. "What is your name?"

"Veronica."

She gave no last name.

"Is anyone following?"

In the rearview mirror, Matthew caught the driver's eye. "Mr. Jones?"

The man checked the rearview mirror and both side mirrors. "I don't think so. There are a couple of cars, but nothing that looks unusual and no one too close. 'Course, I'm not exactly sure what I'm looking for."

"Should we all look?" Matthew couldn't help but grin at Esther's question. She always tried to be helpful.

There was a pause before the muffled voice sounded from the back again. "Best not to make a big deal of it. Don't turn around and stare everywhere. Just let the driver keep an eye out."

"We will do what we can, Veronica." Where were his manners? Matthew shook his head at his failing and fingered his thin black suspenders. None of them had introduced themselves. It was a little odd, since she was concealed in the back, but surely she would want to know their names. "I am sorry I have not said before, but my name is Matthew Yoder, and in the front seat is my *schwester—ach*, sister—Esther. Our driver is Mr. Jones."

"It really is wonderful to meet you, but I don't think I should pop up yet. How long have we been on the road? Thirty minutes?" The voice didn't warble anymore, and she sounded more sure of herself. Perhaps she was beginning to get comfortable with them.

Matthew checked the clock on the dashboard. "*Jah*, about that. And we have another hour to go to our town, Bent Grass."

Esther turned sideways in her seat. "Matthew, could we stop? We could use something to eat and a beverage, and for sure and for certain, our extra passenger could as well." She looked out the windshield as if surveying the area. "If

I remember the route correctly, and we are not far off our usual road, even with our detour, then there is a restaurant coming up."

"I'm sorry to pester." A shuffling sound came from the back cargo area. "But would you check again if anyone has been following or looks the least bit interested in us?"

Mr. Jones glanced in the mirrors again. "I don't think so."

"What about stopping, Veronica? You could ride up here with us then," Matthew asked.

"Yes, if you're sure we're not being followed."

As the driver turned back toward the main road and the restaurant, Matthew leaned forward. "This must be the most interesting fare you have ever had in your Amish taxi."

Mr. Jones chuckled. "Yeah, the Amish are usually a pretty quiet bunch."

He turned into the parking lot and chose a spot that faced the building. Matthew hopped out first, being careful to lift his foot enough so that he didn't stumble again. There didn't seem to be any danger here, but he didn't want to look a fool in front of their pretty passenger. He hobbled around to the back and opened the doors to find the woman named Veronica peeking through the suitcases.

She rose to her knees and peered around his suitcase and through the window, surveying the entire area slowly and carefully. Then, she stepped out and stretched her legs. "I was getting pretty cramped back there, but it doesn't seem I can thank you enough for your rescue at the bus station." She spun back to the van to grab her cross-body bag, and Matthew caught a pleasant scent of fresh apples coming from her shoulder-length strawberry-blond hair.

"Maybe we can introduce ourselves properly now." He shook her hand according to the *Englisch* tradition. The softness of her skin under his fingers startled him. "I am Matthew Yoder."

Esther stepped up beside Matthew. "I am his sister, Esther. 'Tis a pleasure to meet you, and I am glad we could be of help."

Matthew moved back to allow Mr. Jones to come forward, mindful that he didn't step in his usual odd fashion and draw attention to his lame foot. "No problem at all," confirmed the driver. "I'll lead in. Would that be helpful?"

"And I will bring up the rear." Matthew quickly completed the plan as he gestured for both Esther and Veronica to go in front of him.

Could he hide his handicap from Veronica? But why bother? They would drop her wherever she needed to go, and he would never see her again. Still, he had an indescribable desire to appear as a whole and strong man in front of her. As she stepped in front of him, he turned to scan the parking lot one more time and then followed the group into the restaurant, fighting hard to walk like a normal, able-bodied man.

Amish. How had she ended up in the vehicle with a couple of Amish people? It was awkward and difficult, and Veronica wanted to kick herself for not paying attention to Matthew's straw hat, suspenders and unusual pants back at the bus station. But would it have mattered? He had been her only way out of there alive.

She walked in front of him into the little restaurant, trying her best to appear normal to any onlooker. Perhaps she should have asked them to park around back, but then she would have had to give a reason. This way, at least, the van was off the road, in case her pursuers were looking for her to be on the go. And with no one in the van, it might not even be noticed. Sometimes, it seemed safer to stop running and let the pursuers drive on past.

Inside, she and Esther went straight to the facilities. Veronica stared at herself in the warped mirror, running her fingers through her hair, which had been mussed en route, and then tried to straighten out her drab gray shirt. Realizing it was no use, she left with the other woman to slip into a booth in the back corner. From there, she could see the door as well as out the windows.

A handful of other customers dotted the dining area, and cars came and went at the attached gas station. But it didn't seem that they had been followed. For the first time since she had learned of the prison break, Veronica allowed herself a deep breath. All those miles down the road, the only passengers her pursuers might have seen in the minivan were the Amish plus the driver. There was no way to know for sure, but perhaps her stalkers did not know which vehicle had provided her escape. There were a lot of minivans on the road.

What now? She'd never been around the Amish, but she was certain they didn't have cell phones with them. The driver probably had one since he didn't seem to be Amish, but she didn't want to borrow it and then have that conversation with the deputy marshal in front of a bunch of strangers. How in the world would she explain her situation? She scrambled for a plan. As soon as she could, she would find a private phone and make the call to law enforcement. Then, it would be best to figure out a place to lay low while she waited for the marshal to rescue her. *Again.*

The driver—she couldn't remember his name now—and Matthew found her and Esther at the table. Each of the men was carrying a tray of hamburgers, fries and drinks. Her stomach growled at the amazing aroma of fried food wafting her way. Suddenly, she remembered her noodles in the microwave back at home. Had she removed them from the contraption? She couldn't recall, but there was nothing to be done about it now.

Matthew slid into the booth and placed a burger in front of her. "Is this okay?"

"Definitely. It looks delicious, and I haven't had lunch." She gingerly unwrapped the paper as she surveyed the front of the restaurant through the windows. No one new had arrived.

Esther took her hamburger and french fries and placed them on the table but didn't open the wrapper. "We thank the Lord for our food before we eat," she explained. "But it is a silent prayer. You may join if you wish."

Prayer. Of course. Veronica should have figured since they were Amish. "Uh..." She began to stutter out a response, but the three bowed their heads. Gazing down at her hamburger, Veronica made a conscious effort to think *thank You, Lord.*

She continued to stare at her food, counting her fries, until her Amish rescuers raised their heads and began to eat.

Matthew looked at her over the top of his drink. "Are you alright after being jostled around in the back with the luggage?"

"Yes, I think so. Although it feels good to stretch and get upright again." She dipped a french fry into a little container of ketchup.

"Where are you headed? We can drive you."

Worry lines creased the skin around Matthew's rich brown eyes. This was the first opportunity she'd had to examine her rescuer, with his dark brown hair and the handsome angles of his face. He seemed to want to ask more—a lot more—but he didn't. And what could she say? She couldn't tell them the whole truth. There was no way she would endanger these fine people. "Yeah, about that…" Her mind spun for something to say. But she had avoided people for so long that she was rusty at conversation. Her online persona was what she was used to, but she didn't want to give that away until she could evaluate her situation and figure out what to do next. Preferably, Matthew and Esther would never even know about Penelope Cupcake.

Sitting next to her in the booth, Esther put a gentle hand on Veronica's forearm. "How else can we help you?"

The warmth and concern in the Amish woman's face was such that Veronica had not seen since the death of her mother, and tears pricked the back of her eyes. Her heart ached to unload her entire predicament. Suddenly, an unexpected thought flashed into her mind. Would she be as safe, if not more so, with these Amish people than she would be with the US Marshal?

"You've already helped me so much. I don't want to be a burden."

"*Ach*, you are no trouble. We are glad to help someone in need." Matthew sipped his drink. "Where can we take you? Are you headed to a family member or a friend?"

"Uh, I can just stay here, so you can get on your way. I'll call for someone to pick me up." There was no telling how long the marshal might take to get there, but she had been in worse predicaments than having to wait in a restaurant.

"*Nee*, we cannot leave you here," Esther said, and startled upright at the notion. "Do you have a phone to call your friend?"

Veronica's stomach soured, and she dropped her burger back onto the flattened paper. What could she say? She didn't want to be untruthful with these people, who seemed so kind and helpful. She felt like she had been lying for twenty years. In many ways, she had been, with the goal of protecting her own life. Now, to admit the truth, the *real* truth, would be a betrayal of all the witness protection program had done for her and her sisters.

"N-no. No phone. I forgot it back at my apartment. I had to leave in a rush." She pulled her go bag closer to her on the booth's bench seat, as if its presence would provide the security and comfort she longed for.

Their driver pulled his phone out of his pocket and handed it to her. "Here. Take mine. Make your phone call while I get our ice cream. They have our order ready at the counter." He watched her until she took the cell phone from him.

"Thank you." She stared at the phone in her hand, her mind summoning up the telephone number for the US Marshal, the number she was to call if she was ever in danger. Yet, how could she dial it and reveal her secret to Matthew and Esther?

THREE

There was definitely something odd about the woman.

Matthew took his small bowl of vanilla ice cream from Mr. Jones and glanced at Veronica again. A crease had formed in between her delicate eyebrows, and her gaze darted from car to car in the parking lot. She seemed genuinely scared—terrified, even—of something or *someone*. Was it the woman he saw at the bus station? The one with the dark eyes? Why had she shot at their passenger?

How could someone be so evil as to cause another to run for her life?

He shoved his spoon into his dessert as he watched Veronica dig deep into her bowl and push an oversize bite into her mouth. She was avoiding talking, both on the phone to whomever she needed to call, as well as to them in response to their questions about where she was going. Apparently, stalling was the name of her game.

Mr. Jones gestured toward the phone that Veronica had deposited on the table. "Did you get ahold of your friend?"

She only nodded as she scanned the parking lot again.

Matthew heard gravel crunching from outside as a new vehicle arrived at the restaurant. He thought nothing of it until he saw Veronica's eyes grow wide. Her forehead scrunched into many fine wrinkles as she seemed to disappear down into her seat, almost below the booth.

"What is it?" He spun to look out the window, half expecting to see that same woman from the bus station.

"Can we go?" Veronica's voice was tinged with panic, forcing Matthew to turn back to her before he could survey the entire parking lot.

Esther tucked a stray strand of hair back into her *kapp*, her hand trembling. She seemed scared as well, but it was probably in reaction to Veronica's alarm. "Mr. Jones? Are we ready to *goh*?"

"Sure can be, if we need to."

"I would appreciate it." Veronica kept her voice low, although Matthew couldn't see any danger right around them. Perhaps it was instinct, although where she had picked up such survival mechanisms he had no idea.

"*Jah*. 'Tis time." He looked to Veronica once again, trying to communicate as much care and assurance in his gaze as he could muster. "What would be best for you?"

"Could you three go on out to the van? Get in line for the drive-through. I'll go out that side door—" she nodded to a door to her right, on the other side of the ordering counter "—and then I'll come to you. We'll get on the road from there."

"Will do." Matthew scooted out of the booth after Mr. Jones and let his *schwester* go in front of him to the door. There would be no hiding his handicap now, although he made great effort not to limp. Still, after more than a decade, his gait couldn't be altered. He had a lame foot, and there was nothing he could do about it.

He turned to see Veronica walking with knees bent, probably trying to make herself shorter than everyone else. She weaved around customers, always with a quiet "excuse me," but she was obviously trying not to be seen through the front windows. A sudden palpitation rose up in Matthew's chest as he headed toward the front door without her. It wasn't just curiosity about her background. There was something intriguing in her vivacious green eyes that made him want to know more about her.

As he opened the door for Mr. Jones and Esther, he uttered a silent prayer. *Gott, put a hedge of protection around us all. Make us invisible to whomever is after Veronica.* Shame struck him that it had taken him this long to think to pray for her, although her situation was quite unique and something he had never experienced before.

With one last glance into the restaurant, he saw that Veronica had disappeared. They arrived at the van, and Matthew slid into his seat and shut the door as the driver put the vehicle into Reverse. A moment later, they slowly approached the drive-through at the side of building. Mr. Jones took his place in the line of cars, careful to leave enough space in front of the van so he could turn out of the line whenever needed. Meanwhile, Matthew leaned forward and craned his neck to check all around the vehicle for Veronica. When they were one car away from the squawk box, she stepped out from behind an arborvitae tree near the line. A smile stretched across his face with the appearance of the red-haired beauty, and for the briefest of moments, all danger was forgotten as their eyes met.

As he leaned sideways to see between the two front seats of the minivan, he saw the little boy in the back seat of the sedan in front of them poke his older sister in the shoulder. Both stared as Veronica picked her way through the landscaping toward their van. Oblivious to the children's curiosity, she darted her eyes around the drive-through line and the parking lot beyond.

When the car in front finished ordering and started to move past the intercom speaker. Mr. Jones swiveled in his seat. "What do I do? I don't want to place an order and then leave it."

Matthew eyed the car in front and then looked again at Veronica. "*Nee*, just inch forward. Here she comes."

He pulled the side door open, and before the minivan could move half a foot farther, she clambered inside, the odor of exhaust wafting over him and into the seat against the window. She dug in her bag and retrieved a green sweat-shirt, efficiently pulling it on over her long-sleeve shirt. As she grabbed Mr. Jones's baseball cap, which was on the console in between the front seats, she asked, "Mind if I borrow this a moment?" Without waiting for an answer, she tucked up her red hair , then slapped the hat on her head and slouched down in the seat.

With apparent effort, she changed the look on her face instantly, from fear to something akin to nonchalance. Matthew stared in amazement. Apparently, she had no end of tricks in her bag. In those few seconds, Veronica had trans-formed herself from a neat-and-tidy grown woman to the appearance of a surly teenager. "Let's go," she murmured.

Mr. Jones eased the minivan out of the drive-through line and headed toward the road, in the direction of Bent Grass, and Matthew and Esther's home. Matthew forced himself to look out the front windshield, to act natural, but his mind flailed for an explanation to this odd behavior.

Picking up speed to the posted limit, Mr. Jones glared at Veronica in the rearview mirror. "Something is definitely wrong here. Who is after you and why?"

Matthew fiddled with the straw hat he held in his hands and refused to look at their extra passenger. Her eyes were so vivid and vivacious that he'd rather hear her answer without any thoughts of her beauty polluting his mind.

In his peripheral vision, though, he could see that she continued to stare out the window. Was she checking for danger? Or was she avoiding the question? But on these rolling Indiana back roads, there hadn't been another vehicle for miles.

Esther's gentle voice sounded from the front passenger seat. "It could be helpful to know a little bit about you. *Ach*, that is all we want—to help."

"I know, and I appreciate all you've done." Veronica's sharp intake of breath ricocheted around the van. "You've probably saved my life."

"All life is valued by *Gott*." Matthew couldn't keep silent any longer. He turned to look at her. She met his gaze, sorrow radiating from her.

Matthew strained to hear her next words, her voice soft and low as if she was talking only to herself. "It's not like they're going to tell anybody."

Whatever this woman's secrets were, she wanted to keep them that way...

Matthew knew his *schwester* and the elderly driver had the patience of Job, so he kept his mouth shut and practiced his own tolerance of waiting. Silence traveled with them for the next several miles. Eventually, Veronica spoke.

"Twenty years ago, when I was only ten years old, I witnessed a kidnapping ring working a department store. The woman, Nadia Popov, also murdered my parents. I testified and helped to put her in jail." She paused and swallowed hard. "Apparently, she's out now. I didn't recognize the man, but the woman at the bus station was the leader of the trafficking ring."

Matthew inhaled sharply. His chest felt exactly the same

as the time a two-by-four had fallen during a barn raising and hit him square in the sternum. There had to be more to the story. He held his breath, waiting for her to continue. A person couldn't just drop a bombshell like that and not tell the rest.

A tear squeezed out of the corner of Veronica's eye, and he felt moisture sting the insides of his eyelids in sympathy. What would it be like to be on the run from someone who, most likely, wanted you dead? He wasn't sure he could imagine it. She hadn't done anything wrong and, it seemed, had, in fact, done the right thing. But now, she suffered the consequences of another person's sins.

He reached for her hand, intending a squeeze of understanding, but suddenly the van jerked forward, and he grabbed the back of the front seat to steady himself. Veronica dug her feet into the floorboards, but her body still swayed with the motion. She stared straight ahead while Matthew spun to see behind.

"A black sedan," he whispered.

The vehicle tapped the bumper again, and all four occupants of the Amish taxi flailed forward, as the road led them downhill.

Veronica nodded, the pinch between her eyebrows deepening.

Mr. Jones turned his head toward the back as much as he could while still keeping his eyes on the road. "Now what? Maybe I should just pull off and let them go by. The impatience of some people these days astounds me."

"No." Veronica's strident voice made Matthew's pulse pound even harder. "Don't pull off. That's what they want. We must keep going."

Matthew turned back to find her staring at him with intense worry. "*Ach*, the window tint is so heavy, I cannot see if it is a *mensch* or a *maedel* or even if there is more than one person."

Even as he finished his sentence, the vehicle pulled up alongside the minivan. Veronica crouched down farther in her seat and then grabbed for the handrest as the black sedan rammed into the side of the van. Mr. Jones gripped the steering wheel, fighting to stay on the road as they sped up a small hill.

Esther whimpered from the front seat.

Moments later, the black car pulled away and then returned to bump the minivan again.

"Keep going," Veronica choked out in a whisper.

The car moved away again as if preparing for a third blow. But as they crested the rise, a box truck approached in the black vehicle's lane. It quickly slowed its speed and dropped back behind the minivan.

The respite didn't last long. As soon as the truck passed, the sedan roared forward with a vengeance, steering its front corner almost directly into the minivan. Mr. Jones clenched the wheel, but the force of the impact pushed the right tires into the dirt on the side of the country highway. A police vehicle, lights flashing, sailed over the next hill and down toward them. Matthew sat up straighter. Did they dare to stop, or was there some way to summon the help of the officer as they passed?

But as he turned back to check the position of the black sedan, it pulled in behind them and then turned onto a side road and sped away, leaving only a trail of exhaust and swirling leaves in its wake. Mr. Jones, still fighting to stay on the road, bounced over a large piece of tire that had been discarded on the side of the road.

Matthew grasped the back of Esther's seat to stay upright. As the minivan's front tires hit a log, it shuddered, completely off the road. The van jerked to a violent stop, Matthew's head hitting the soft back of the headrest.

"Esther, are you alright?" His *schwester* had flopped forward as well.

"*Jah*, I am well. What about Mr. Jones?"

"I'm fine." The driver sat upright and rubbed his shoulder.

A low moan emanated from the seat beside Matthew. He spun to see Veronica sitting up from where she must have hit her head against the window. "How are you? Hurt? You were jostled around without a seat belt on."

"I don't know." She pulled her hand away from her forehead to reveal an ugly gash.

"*Ach*, you are bleeding." He retrieved his handkerchief from his pants pocket and handed it to her. "We should seek medical help."

Mr. Jones put the van in Reverse and then pulled back on the road. A loud clunking sounded from the underside of the vehicle. "And we probably need a mechanic. I'm not sure I can get you home." He continued to rub his shoulder. "If I remember correctly, there's an urgent-care center a little way down the road, and there's a collision-repair center near there as well."

Matthew checked behind them. "The other vehicle seems to be gone, praise *Gott*. So drive to the medical center. We can get it all taken care of at once." *As long as they did not run into more trouble on the road.* But it was best that he not say that aloud.

Twenty minutes later, with the minivan rattling and thunking down the road, Mr. Jones pulled into the parking lot of a medical center in the middle of a strip mall. Veronica's head ached, but it was manageable, especially since the danger seemed to be gone.

For now.

She slid from her seat and planted her feet on the sidewalk, glad to be out of the vehicle. Matthew confirmed with his sister that she would go with Mr. Jones to the collision-repair center across the street and then he held the door open for her at the clinic. As he guided her by the elbow, he leaned in and said quietly, "I will be your eyes and ears in the waiting room. Just in case."

"Thank you." She managed to keep what felt like an even expression on her face. But the way Matthew blinked so rapidly and then cleared his throat belied his nervousness. She admired his attempt to hide his handicap, but she had noticed right away, back at the bus station, that one leg was shorter than the other.

Clearly, he wanted to protect her, but could he be helpful if her safety came down to a matter of brute strength and ability?

"Name?" The plump woman behind the counter looked at Veronica expectantly.

Oh, no. Which name should she give? If she gave the moniker WITSEC had given her—Veronica Williams—she would be on the grid. It seemed that Nadia Popov knew that name since the woman, somehow, had found her. That meant her location would be easy to find once this clinic put her into their computer system. If she gave a different name, perhaps she could stay hidden from Popov for a bit longer.

But Matthew was standing next to her, and she had already introduced herself, even before the restaurant stop, with her current alias. How would she explain a different name to him? Within the space of just the last couple of hours, she had become intrigued by him. With dismay, she admitted to herself that it mattered what he thought. His calm and faith in the face of adversity also drew her in and made her want to know more about his Amish religion. But was his impression of her more important than her safety?

She leaned over the counter to be heard as she kept her voice low. "Elizabeth Kane."

A glance at Matthew's raised eyebrows revealed his surprise. She just shook her head slightly toward the waiting area to indicate that she would explain later. He immediately adopted a look of disinterest, turned and ambled toward a chair. Hope rose within Veronica. It seemed he was catching on. Perhaps he would be more helpful than she had thought.

Done at the desk, she took the chair next to him, grateful that they were away from the door and front window, but were located where they could see everything. "At least the minivan won't be out front, in case the people that drove us off the road are still looking."

Matthew twirled his straw hat in his hands. "*Jah*, we are hidden here at the clinic." He cleared his throat quietly then pierced her with his rich brown eyes, a playful smile bouncing about his lips. "What is your *real* name?"

She stared at a poster on the opposite wall. "Veronica is actually a middle name, and the name I checked in with is my legal first name, the one that's on all the documents." Another lie. It came so automatically now, it scared her sometimes. Her parents had taught their daughters to always tell the truth, but her whole life had been a fabrication since she had entered WITSEC twenty years ago. The rationale was that it was all for her own safety and the safety of her two sisters, who were hidden somewhere deep within the system as well.

Veronica could feel Matthew staring at her a little too long for comfort, but she refused to look at him. Yes, she was fascinated by him, but that didn't mean she could trust him.

"*Ach*, I don't remember now. Where did you say you were from?"

She wanted to cut her eyes at him but kept it to herself. He knew good and well she had never said where she was from. "I've been in Fort Wayne for several years." Worry seized her throat and kept her from answering. She had lived in hiding for so many years and her entire background had been changed. It wasn't something that had been easy to get used to.

Despite having sisters, the US Marshal had made up a new background that painted her as an only child whose parents had been killed in a helicopter crash. Her handler must have had a flair for a suspenseful story. She didn't know anyone who knew anyone who had been in a helicopter crash, let alone flown in a helicopter. Eventually, she had spent two years at a community college and then worked in retail sales at the mall while she started her blog under her nom de plume. It was so different from the way she had actually grown up, at least to age ten, that it was difficult to remember. And it certainly didn't seem fair to her sisters, who had been a cherished part of her life up until that fateful moment.

"What do you do there?" Compassion tinged Matthew's voice.

"I worked in a women's clothing store at the mall." Well, it *used* to be true. She unraveled a bit of thread from the edge of the handle of her bag. Who would she be at the end of this, if she survived? Would she be able to keep her identity, or would she be forced to remake herself again? The bigger question was not whether her name would change but if the very essence of her would be altered in some way.

"Elizabeth." A nurse stood at an interior door.

When Veronica didn't move, Matthew elbowed her. "Isn't that you?"

She stood quickly, grasping her bag. "Yeah, thanks. You'll be here?"

"*Jah.* In prayer." He stood and took a chair closer to the door as she was ushered back to an examination room.

Inside, she surveyed her surroundings, the way she had trained herself to do several years ago. White cabinets with a white counter flanked one entire wall. An examining table stretched the length of the opposite wall, a blood-pressure cuff and a defibrillator on a wheeled pole near the head of the bed. A third wall sported a variety of medical posters.

The nurse quickly took her vitals, making notes on a tablet. "You were in a car accident?"

"Sort of. We went off the road, and I hit my head on the window."

"Blurry vision?"

"No."

The nurse held up a finger out in front of Veronica's face. "Follow—"

A knock sounded as the door opened and another nurse poked her head in the room. "Glenda, you have a phone call. Urgent." Then she disappeared.

"I'm sorry. I'm sure it won't take long. I'll be right back." She hurried out.

Alone, Veronica leaned back on the crinkling paper and pillow. Exhaustion consumed her. Eyes closed, she savored the silence and stillness. She was accustomed to solitude after so many years alone, and the frenetic activity of the afternoon had frazzled her.

A moment later, she heard the door open again. Reluctant to jostle herself from the momentary rest and sit up, she continued to lie back. Three seconds ticked by, and the nurse didn't speak. Veronica laid her arm over her forehead. She must be imagining things now, and she hadn't heard the door at all. So many years of hiding and now running seemed to be taking their toll on her mental health.

The sound of a lid creaking open near her head startled her. Veronica popped her eyes open just in time to see a different nurse leaning over her, the paddles of the defibrillator in her hands. The woman scowled at her, a look of venom in her dark eyes.

In a split second, the woman lunged at Veronica and pressed the paddles down toward her chest. She instinctually lifted her arms in a protective stance, pushing the attack away. Without touching her skin, the paddles had minimal effectiveness, but she could hear the crackle of electricity that told her they were charged and ready to be used.

The nurse lifted the paddles higher and attacked again, pushing against Veronica's forearms. Inch by inch, she forced them down closer to Veronica's body. Exhaustion, both physical and mental, consumed her. But fresh adrenaline pulsed through her, giving her added strength. She grabbed the woman's wrists, squeezing as tight as she could in her weakened state, to hold her off.

Veronica peered at what she could see of the assailant's face behind a green surgical mask. Dark hair was tucked into a cap, but she could still tell it was the woman from all those years ago, the one who had escaped prison. A lot of time had passed, and she had aged considerably, but Veronica still knew her malicious eyes. *Nadia Popov.*

Popov, her eyes cut into slits with the efforts of her attack, continued to push the paddles closer, taking advantage of her superior position.

Veronica tried to draw a deep breath, oxygenating to build additional strength. But if she expanded her chest to inhale, she would be closer to the paddles. Her lungs seemed to seize as she hiccuped with half a breath. Perspiration trickled down her back.

"Matthew!" How far away was he? Would he be able to hear her? Where was everybody?

The woman jerked her wrist free to grab a wad of gauze from a nearby counter. She shoved it in Veronica's mouth as she opened it to call for help again. The fabric squares immediately absorbed all the moisture in her mouth. There was no way she could scream for assistance now. Veronica chewed on the gauze, trying to work it out of her mouth, still gripping one of the nurse's wrists.

Popov jerked free. With a fresh hold on the paddles, she lunged at Veronica again. Veronica shot her arms up to ward off the attack. But Popov was increasingly stronger.

Fatigue consumed her. Would this be it, then? The end of her running and hiding would come in a place dedicated to health and well-being?

She worked the wad of gauze, now soaked with her saliva, up to her lips. With one last burst of energy, she spit the wad in the face of the nurse. It hit her surgical mask and left a wet spot before it dropped onto Veronica's chest.

Anger spread across Popov's face. Brute strength burned a hatred in the woman's eyes. Electricity crackled, and Veronica glanced down to see her attacker moving the paddles up and to within an inch of her head. Despair consumed her, and her endurance waned. The end of her strength was a breath away.

In a moment, the electrified paddles would strike her body. After twenty years of hiding, death was imminent.

FOUR

Matthew's attention roamed the waiting room, and one thing was abundantly clear to him.

Englischers were an odd folk.

Every single one of them seemed to have an abnormal attachment to their cell phones. They couldn't get a drink of water or check in at the desk or take a child to the restroom without bringing their phone. Of course, he'd heard about it from other Amish who got out more than he did, but to see it with his own eyes? He rubbed a hand over his chin and put his hat back on. Apparently those gadgets served a purpose, but these people acted like they were attached to their hands. Well, what was their saying? To each their own? Or as he had heard a young person say in the general store a few weeks ago—*you do you*.

The door that had swallowed Veronica opened, but it was only a nurse to call back another patient. Matthew ran his hands up and down his suspenders. Was she alright back there? Were the nurses taking good care of her and treating her properly? He wished he could have gone with her, but that would have been quite inappropriate. An Amishman in an exam room with a strange *Englisch* woman? One he had just met a couple of hours ago? *Nee*, extremely inadvisable. He would have had a visit from the bishop over that, for sure and for certain.

Still, though, the thought nagged him. Was she okay? Was she *safe*?

"Matthew?" Esther's gentle voice startled him out of his reverie, and he turned to see that she and Mr. Jones had returned. "Is Veronica in with the doctor?"

"Jah." With one last long look at the door, he turned to his *schwester* and Mr. Jones as they claimed seats. "How is the taxi?"

"The mechanic did some fast tweaking, so it's working better and can get us back to Bent Grass. But it'll need more body work. I'll get that figured out later."

"Gut. Denki for getting that taken care of."

"No worries, Matthew." Mr. Jones paused and skewered him with a look. "The bigger question is what to do with our stowaway. I can call someone with my phone, but since you're Amish…well, I just can't figure who you would call. No other folks in your community would have a phone to be able to receive your call."

"Jah, and it sounds like she has nowhere to go." Esther tugged her chair a little closer.

Their driver continued his argument. "She's not your problem. In fact, it sounds like she brings plenty of problems with her. Maybe she can call someone. Surely she has connections somewhere."

Esther touched Matthew's arm. "You feel an obligation to this *maedel*?"

Matthew hesitated. Did he? An indescribable pull tugged at his insides as he yanked off his hat and ran his hand over his hair. He could not leave a *maedel* stranded with no place to go. "I am an Amish man who lives a life of faith. I will do what I can to help the *maedel*." She was so fascinating—

with her mysterious background, her resourcefulness, and her red-blond hair that smelled of freshly baked apple pie— and he was not ready to drop her off somewhere and go home to the cold, lonely *haus*. *Jah*, his *schwester* lived there with him, and she was *wunderbaar-gut*, but that was the problem. She was his *schwester*. He wanted a different relationship.

Yet what could he really offer a woman, as a disabled person?

He'd lived with his disability for nigh on fifteen years, and yet it still seemed an adjustment to his everyday life. Some mornings he woke up expecting to bound out of bed onto two good legs.

At a mere twenty years old, young Matthew had rushed into the sky-high flames eagerly consuming his family's *haus*. Despite smoke inhalation and his shirtsleeve catching fire, he had been unable to get his *daed* and *mamm* out. With tears streaming down his face as smoke mingled with frustration and grief, blocking his vision, he was forced to jump out a second-floor window, shattering his leg. He sought all the proper medical care, but it didn't heal correctly, leaving him with one leg shorter and weaker. Esther had *kumme* out as soon as she saw the flames. But what if he had lost her as well? Sometimes, even now, she accused Matthew of being an old mother hen in his protectiveness.

He rubbed the back of his neck as the image of the *Englisch* red-haired beauty rose unbidden in his mind. What could he actually do to protect Veronica? No woman wanted a disabled man by her side. He had learned that lesson well in the aftermath of the fire when the Amish girl he had been courting had ended their budding romance a week after the smoke had cleared. Between the trauma of the fire, his grief over the death of his parents and the difficulties of adjusting to his new handicap, plus the burden of having to provide for himself and care for his younger sister, the girl had had enough. To add insult to injury, she had been unkind about his impediment, questioning his future and whether he would be able to do the physical labor required of an Amish husband. The harsh expression on her face had told him everything he needed to know.

No woman would want him now. His dream of marriage and a family had died in that fire.

They had rebuilt the *haus*, but it wasn't that easy to re-build a life.

Mr. Jones stood. "I'm going to find a vending machine. Do you want anything?"

"Nee, denki." Esther scooted closer to Matthew as the driver walked away. "What makes you so pensive, *mein bruder*? I appreciate that you want to help the *maedel*, but you are not ultimately responsible for her."

Thoughts swirled in his mind, and before he could re-think it, the words tumbled out in the safety of the private conversation with his *schwester*. "Would it be disloyal to *Mamm* and *Daed* if I married? If I moved on with life?"

Esther simply listened, giving him space to speak.

"The most honoring thing would be to live in a moment from fifteen years ago, suspended in time. Before the fire. Wouldn't it?"

Suddenly, the lines around her eyes crinkled with a smile of compassion as she patted his hand, the same way *Mamm* used to comfort him. "What do you think?"

What *did* he think? The difficult question plagued him.

Life as a bachelor all these years had been just fine. *Jah*, watching his friends get married and have *boppli* had been difficult. But he enjoyed his bookstore and his home, and the occasional barn raising. He had thought he was content.

But now, this *maedel*, odd as her situation seemed to be,

had appeared in his life. Something mysterious and compelling drew him out, making him want to protect in a way he hadn't before. The question he thought he had settled had suddenly resurrected itself. Would he be able to take care of a family, especially if he had a wife who believed in him?

The antiseptic odor of the medical office tickled, and Matthew ran a hand over his face. He was putting the buggy in front of the horse. This poor *maedel* had enough danger to deal with in the present moment, and he was leading her to the bishop for a marriage ceremony? His shoulders slumped. She wouldn't want him, anyway.

Besides, he was just a peaceful Amish man whose only weapon was a hunting rifle, and it would definitely be against his faith, not to mention the trouble he'd be in with the bishop, if he tried to use it for any other purpose. His wits were his only weapon. And while he was, admittedly, well-read—an occupational hazard of owning a bookstore—that didn't necessarily translate to being *gut* at protecting someone from a physical attack.

Esther watched him, waiting for his answer.

"*Ach*, I do not know what I think, except that I need to continue to pray over it."

A faint sound reached him over the noise of the people talking in the waiting room. Was that yelling? The sound of trauma? Someone was having a difficult time in the exam room. Matthew shot up a silent prayer for comfort and healing for whoever it was.

He ran his gaze over the magazines arranged in a display near the front desk. Nothing there appealed to him, and, in fact, would probably prompt a comment from his *schwester* if he picked one up. If only he had brought in the latest copy of *The Budget*, the Amish community newspaper, but he had left it in his bag in the minivan. Mr. Jones returned with a plastic bottle of some blue drink, and as Matthew determined to ask him for the keys, the wailing sound hit again. This time it was more intense.

He looked around to see if anyone else heard it and crashed his gaze into Esther's startled eyes. "You hear that?"

"*Jah.* Someone is in distress."

Surely, Veronica was safe here. He couldn't figure any way she could be discovered. But he lived a simple and humble life. What did he know of running for safety?

An alarm pinged in his brain, making his heart race. He stood abruptly and stepped toward the door that led to the examination rooms, his gait uneven. He spun back to Esther. "That sounds like Veronica. I'm going to find her."

Matthew shoved aside his sense of propriety. After yanking the door open, he barreled through. The wailing grew louder. Would he be in time?

With a quick intake of oxygen, Veronica released another loud cry for help, unsure she had the strength for any more. Struggling for endurance, she pushed back against her attacker's forearms, the defibrillator paddles within an inch of her head. If they touched her scalp? She would be too dead to hear the sizzling of the electricity.

The woman's eyes opened wide with Veronica's yelling. Keeping one paddle aimed at Veronica's head, she dropped the other to the side of the table and lunged for another thick pad of gauze. She shoved it at Veronica's open mouth. But this time, Veronica thrashed her head to the right, away from the paddle and narrowly avoiding the gauze.

Summoning all the strength she could find and throwing up a quick prayer, Veronica knocked away the defibrillator paddles. One clattered to the floor. Surely someone would hear that and come to her rescue. The other hit the wall, ricocheted off and spun back toward her. She shrunk back. What could just one paddle do to her? Nothing, if she remembered her college science class correctly, but she wasn't going to take any chances. It glanced off her hand, and she jerked away. But the only effect was the pain of impact.

Matthew's kind and gentle demeanor rose in her mind, his rejection of violence, and new energy coursed through her. She hardly knew the handsome Amish man, but he had already offered her, by his presence alone, such a peace and acceptance that a renewed determination to throw off this attacker infused her.

Popov spun toward the counter, flailing about for something new to attack Veronica with, and began yanking open drawers and cabinets. Veronica rolled off the exam table and stopped, hunched over. The room spun crazily about her. The antiseptic smell of the medical office enhanced her dizziness, seeping into her brain and making her vision swim.

The sound of supplies clattering stopped abruptly. Veronica twisted to find the woman's arm raised, a syringe in her hand, with only a few feet of space between them.

"Help!" she hollered again, desperation raising her voice to a new volume.

With Popov and the syringe a few inches away, the exam room door flew open. Not taking her eyes off her attacker, Veronica registered in her peripheral vision Matthew filling the doorway. With two steps, he knocked the syringe out of the woman's hand.

She gasped involuntarily. He had come for her. He had heard her and come to rescue her.

A nurse rushed in behind him. Popov dodged to the left and around her, toward the door.

"*Ach*, are you alright?" Matthew's concern crinkled the corners of his eyes, worry radiating from his presence.

Veronica could only nod as the floor rushed upward, her surroundings spinning again. Her legs weak, she felt Matthew's strong arms about her as everything disappeared into blackness.

FIVE

Light flickered through her eyelids as Veronica became aware of the firm mattress underneath her, the pungent odor of antiseptic and the tingling of the skin on her arms. She heard a man's steady breathing. Maybe Matthew? She hoped so. Why she felt such a belief in him, she couldn't understand. With her own life an artificial creation thanks to the witness protection program, she hadn't been able to trust anyone for several years. She had been remade into a new person, and all vestiges of who she was, or at least who she had been, had been erased. Didn't that mean, then, that she shouldn't be sure of who anyone *really* was? After all, no amount of counseling provided by the US Marshals' office had been able to help her.

The squeak of soles on a linoleum floor approached, and her muscles tensed in anticipation of another attack. But a gentle touch on her shoulder forced her eyes to open a smidge.

A woman's smiling face hovered over her. "Good, you're back with us. How do you feel?"

Veronica swallowed, trying to eliminate some of the dryness. "Like I've been run over. What happened?"

"You fainted. Need some water?" The nurse held a white Styrofoam cup with a bendable straw toward her, and she lifted up on a shoulder to sip the soothing cool liquid. "There's been a lot happening. What do you remember?"

Veronica sank back onto the pillow and turned her head cautiously to see Matthew sitting in a chair a few feet away. The exam room came into focus, the same one she had been in before. Maybe she had never left it. "A car accident. I hit my head. I came here." She paused, scrunching her forehead as she thought through the past hour. "A woman attacked me."

"All correct. And you seem to have come through it unscathed. If you'll give me a few more minutes, we can get you out of here." The nurse examined her, poking, prodding, shining lights at her and asking more questions.

Matthew held his hat in both hands and smiled at her encouragingly through the ordeal. "I can leave if you'd like."

But all Veronica could do was shake her head. It was nothing inappropriate, and his presence soothed her frazzled nerves.

With a polite knock, the door swung open, and a police officer entered the exam room. Veronica cringed at the uniform, instantly trying to plaster on her face what felt like a neutral expression to hide her fear of law-enforcement involvement in her WITSEC identity. "Who called the police?" She couldn't keep the wobble out of her voice.

The nurse tossed her a curious look. "I had one of the office staff call nine-one-one as soon as we saw you were attacked." She nodded toward the officer. "When I'm done, you can stay here for some privacy while you give the officer your statement."

Palpitations beat within her chest as a sour taste rose in her throat. Had she been conscious, she would have insisted she was alright and not to call the police. Her transition to WITSEC all those years ago included strict instructions to communicate directly with the US Marshals' office. They were responsible for her and would protect her. Not local law enforcement. Not only had she not completed the call to them yet, but the police officer was also already there, talking to Matthew in low tones.

She would have to talk to him, but maybe she shouldn't put off calling her handler. Avoiding reality a bit longer would have soothed her, but when she could find a private phone, she would make the call.

The nurse finished securing a bandage on her forehead, and when she stepped away, Veronica glimpsed it in the mirror on the opposite wall. At least it wasn't huge, and the woman said it could come off in another day. With final directions, the nurse left her and Matthew alone with the officer.

The policeman smiled with compassion as he pulled out a notepad. "Can you tell me what happened?"

Veronica fisted the hem of her shirt as her palm slicked with moisture. "Not much, Officer. The nurse stepped out of the room. I had my eyes closed to rest when a woman came in and lunged for me with the defibrillator paddles." She briefly explained the struggle and Matthew rescuing her. "That's all I remember."

"So, a woman. Was she tall? Short? Hair color? What was she wearing? Any identifying characteristics like tattoos or piercings or scars?" The officer jotted a note down on his pad.

"I was lying down, and then we were both bent over in the struggle." All true, but a cringe shot through Veronica. It felt like lying. "She had dark hair and dark eyes." She glanced at Matthew, but his expression remained stoic and nonreactive. Was he judging her? Condemning her? Or were the Amish just like that? She pressed her hand to her throat. Why did she care what he thought? As soon as they got out of the clinic, she would be on her own, never to cross paths with him again.

Veronica suppressed a sigh of relief when the officer didn't press her. "So what happened with the woman?"

"She's a fast mover. I can definitely tell you that much. She dodged everyone here trying to stop her and escaped through the back door. She's in the wind, now."

Matthew cleared his throat. "'In the wind'?"

The officer wrote something down. "It means she's gone. No trace of her. She probably had an accomplice waiting in a getaway vehicle." He tucked his notepad into an inside pocket of his jacket and pulled out a business card, which he handed to Veronica. "If you think of anything else, please call."

That would be easier if she hadn't left her cell phone behind, but she didn't plan on contacting him, anyway. When she had been placed into WITSEC, the strict instructions included keeping her true identity and the fact that she was in witness protection as secret as possible. *Tell no one.* Or at least, tell as few people as possible. That included law enforcement. The Deputy US Marshal had said that they would handle everything for her. Too many people don't know how to keep a secret, she had been admonished, and she would be putting her very life at risk if she had loose lips.

Veronica accepted the card and allowed herself a deep breath when the officer had gone. An ache rose in her middle. She wanted to trust him, to tell him everything so he could help find Nadia Popov and whoever was helping her. Then safety could return. But she couldn't violate the conditions of the witness protection program. As the marshal had warned many years ago, she didn't know who that officer might tell and then who that person might tell and so on, until both her identity and her safety were compromised.

A tremor ran through her body. She had already risked too much by confiding in this stranger, Matthew.

Risking a glance in the mirror, she ran her hand over her hair. What a mess she was after the day she had had so far. But he simply stood and smiled at her, his expression warm and encouraging. "Ready?"

She glanced down at the floor, suddenly unable to meet his gaze. Granted, she had only known him for a few hours, but was he still a stranger? In her copious free time, she had read many things, including random definitions in the dictionary. If memory served, a stranger was someone who was neither a friend nor an acquaintance. *An outsider.* Yet, that definition didn't fit Matthew. Not anymore. He was, at the very least, an acquaintance. And with what had happened in the past few hours and what information about herself she had been compelled to share with him, neither was he an outsider.

She forced herself to return his smile, afraid it turned out to be more of a grimace, but he just continued to smile. "Ready to go?"

Veronica nodded. Yes, she was definitely ready to leave that exam room and the clinic. Where she would go, though, was an entirely different question.

Matthew peeked through the door back to the waiting room, checking all around for any dangers, before he held it open wide for Veronica to pass through first. Her reddish-blond hair bounced on her shoulders as she walked in front of him, and he marveled at her strength and resilience. Fending off a potentially deadly attack wasn't something most women encountered on an everyday basis. He thought he had a fair imagination built by many hours of reading, but he had a difficult time imagining the feeling of knowing someone was trying to kill him.

In the waiting room, Esther rushed to Veronica. He recognized her expression as the one that meant she wanted to wrap someone in a warm hug, but she contented herself with holding Veronica's arms in her hands. "*Ach*, we heard you yelling for help all the way out here. How are you? Are you well?" Mr. Jones stood behind her, mirroring Esther's concerned expression.

"I'm alright. Thanks to my rescuer." She turned to flash a small smile at Matthew.

Meeting Esther's pointed gaze, he knew exactly what his younger *schwester* was thinking. But he refused to dwell on the fact that they now had accompanying them a beautiful *maedel* who thought he was a hero. Her appreciation was only temporary. Soon they would drop her off in her *Englisch* world somewhere, and that would be that.

"Is everyone ready to *goh* home?" But as soon as the words were out of his mouth, his brain reminded his heart that one of their passengers no longer had a home.

Now what?

As they left the clinic, they formed a protective circle around Veronica. Matthew glanced around the parking lot, making sure of their surroundings and watching for anyone lurking in or around the cars. Was this what law-enforcement officers felt like all the time? A new feeling of protectiveness surged within him.

Back in the van, Mr. Jones put the key in the ignition but didn't start the vehicle. Instead, he looked in the rearview mirror with a lingering glance at Matthew. Then he turned his focus on Veronica. After a pause, he asked her, "Where can I drop you?"

She stammered, stuttering out an unintelligible answer as she averted her gaze to the outside.

Before she could clarify, Matthew spoke. "Head to our *haus* first, please, Mr. Jones."

A look of relief swept across the driver's face. "No problem," he said as he backed out of the parking spot and headed toward the highway.

"Denki."

Matthew turned to Veronica. He wanted desperately to help her, maybe to prove to himself that he was capable of taking care of someone after he had failed so miserably in taking care of his parents. Maybe because she was pretty and smelled like his favorite dessert, apple pie. Or perhaps just to satisfy his curiosity. Whatever his reason, he didn't have the resources to be able to track down the escaped convict who was stalking her. He couldn't fix her life, which meant he didn't have a lot of options.

But he could offer shelter in his *haus*. It wasn't a big place, and it wasn't fancy like the *Englischers* preferred. She would probably struggle with the Amish lack of electricity. But he had a spare bedroom and indoor plumbing. Propane powered their lights and refrigerator, and Esther could get a hot meal on the table.

"Veronica."

She turned to him with wide azure eyes, nibbling on her lower lip. "Hmm?"

It seemed she had been deep in thought, but Matthew plunged ahead. This could solve what was probably worrying her. "We—" His brain stumbled over his words as she continued to gaze at him. "*Mein schwester*, Esther, and I have an extra room. Why not stay with us?"

"Are you serious?" An expression of surprise flitted across her face. Was she that unaccustomed to demonstrations of caring and generosity that his simple offer startled her? Matthew had suffered mightily with the loss of his parents, but at least he still had his *schwester*.

"*Jah*." Esther rotated in the front seat. "We want to do whatever we can."

Tears sprang into Veronica's eyes. She didn't know what else to do. That much was evident on her face. Esther saw it also, and a moment later, matching tears glistened in his *schwester*'s gaze. "Amish country could be a good place to hide until I can reach my contact. But I don't want to put you out."

"*Nee*, you won't. We want to do this for you."

"I don't want to put you in any danger, either."

Matthew's heart swelled with compassion for the *maedel*. "We trust in the Lord *Gott*. He will protect and guide us." He squeezed his hands together as he glanced out the window. Did he really believe that? *Gott* had not protected his parents in the scorching heat and fiery blaze that had claimed their *haus* and their lives. Matthew had fought the searing heat and choking smoke to save them, but in the end had to get out before the flames claimed him. He had saved his own life but been left with both a permanent limp and some serious doubts. How could a *Gott* who loved and cared for them and supposedly wanted only the best for his people allow Matthew's parents to die in such a horrible tragedy? How could he reconcile the love *Gott* claimed He had for His people with that trauma?

But he couldn't voice those misgivings. Not out loud. Instead, they churned inside him while he plastered on the smile of a contented Amish man and forced himself to return his attention to the *maedel* sitting next to him.

Veronica nodded, and Esther turned back to face the front with a satisfied twist of her shoulders.

Matthew wanted to ask more about Veronica, to get to know her and what her life had been like up until she'd jumped into the back of the minivan. But what was the point? She needed to figure out her problems and move on, back to the *Englisch* world. Under normal circumstances, she would never look twice at him. What was that saying he had heard the *Englisch* use? *Three strikes and you're out.* He was Amish. She was *Englisch*. He had a permanent handicap. And he ran a bookstore that, most definitely, was not a masculine job, like farming or making furniture. He had three strikes. He was out.

After several miles, Bent Grass came into view and soon the minivan drove past the collection of shops, the post office, the schools and the library, as well as a handful of office buildings that made up the little town. Amish and *Englisch* alike farmed the surrounding land, with a farm-implement dealership just out of town that sold both machinery with engines for the *Englisch* farmers and horse-drawn farming equipment for the Amish. Soon, the taxi was back in the countryside, where Amish houses were painted white with green blinds in the windows and clotheslines in the yard.

"Here we are," Mr. Jones announced as he turned down a gravel lane several minutes out of town. A wooden sign announced the livery where Matthew had boarded his horse and left his buggy for the trip.

Matthew paid the old man, including extra for his trouble, and promised to compensate him for whatever repairs would be necessary after being run off the road. Soon, he sat in his buggy, the reins of his horse, Dickens, firmly in grip. It was *gut* to be home, but a pang hit him in the midsection when he thought of how Veronica would love to be going home as well.

Doubting their safety with so many dark sedans on the road that looked like the one that hit the minivan earlier, Matthew tucked Veronica into the back of his buggy with Esther up front. The dark of night quickly consumed the sky, and by the time they reached the *haus*, Veronica had fallen asleep. Esther jiggled her awake just enough to get her inside, where she plodded into the spare bedroom, a borrowed nightgown in one hand, half-asleep already.

With the *maedels* settled inside, Matthew stalked the perimeter of his property. He'd never done anything like that before, but it seemed necessary to make sure all was well. Debating whether to retrieve his hunting rifle and have it on hand, he sat in his recliner in the dark, ready to be vigilant throughout the night.

He knew he wasn't enough for Veronica. But just for to-night, he would pretend.

SIX

Veronica startled awake to bright sunlight streaming through the white sheers at the windows. The heavenly aroma of frying bacon and baking biscuits assaulted her. Her stomach growled in protest. The delicious scents seemed to be a good sign that she was safe.

Raising her arms above her head, she stretched in the comfortable bed. She'd slept so hard that grogginess shadowed her. Through drooping eyelids, she looked around the room at the simple wood furnishings and the plain green window coverings. The four white walls were completely empty except for a lone calendar hanging by a nail. On the bedside table stood a lamp with pretty pastoral pictures on the glass panes of the lampshade. As she looked at it, it struck her that there was no cord to an outlet. A plain green dress with a white apron hung on the door of the wardrobe. A white bonnet hung on a wooden peg.

What had happened yesterday? Was she staying with the Pilgrims?

"Ah, *gut*. You are awake." A dark-haired woman in a bright blue dress with a white apron like the one on the hanger bustled in, rubbing her hands together. *"Gut morge."*

Veronica's mind went blank, and she simply blinked at the Amish woman.

"That means 'good morning.'" The woman smiled and paused in the doorway.

Amish. Yes. It all flooded back—the bus station, the minivan, the Amish brother and sister who helped her escape, the attack in the urgent-care center. This kind woman was Esther, sister to Matthew. It took great effort to feel more awake, but Veronica forced a smile and returned the greeting.

Esther retrieved the bottle-green dress and white apron on the hanger from the wardrobe. "Ready to get dressed in your disguise?"

She swallowed hard. "My what?" Was she supposed to wear that? She did like the green color and often wished she wore more dresses. But it was difficult to find the motivation to put on anything other than yoga pants when she barely left the house and rarely came into contact with anyone. Considering her usual style, or lack thereof, this would definitely change her look.

"*Jah.* Disguise. Matthew had the idea that if you dressed like us Amish, no one would recognize you. You would be safer." Esther fluffed up the skirt. "I agree. He is a *gut* man with very *gut* ideas."

"Well, I can't disagree with that. I'm not sure I'd be alive now if not for hiding in the minivan's trunk."

"Are you hungry?" Esther hung the dress back on the front of the wardrobe. "Matthew and I ate a couple of hours ago, but we saved plenty for you."

Veronica glanced out the window. A couple of hours ago? The sun barely peeked over the horizon right now. How long had they been up? Before she could answer, her stomach growled a reply.

Esther smiled. "*Gut.* I will step out while you get dressed, but I will need to return to attach the skirt to the bodice for you." She motioned to a little dish of straight pins.

Before Veronica could ask what she meant, Esther pulled the door closed behind her.

The petite Amish woman certainly exuded energy in the morning. Veronica pulled back the covers and stood, stretching her arms over her head. She should do some sort of exercise to get her blood flowing so she could keep up with Matthew's sister. After quickly exchanging the nightgown for the separate pieces of the green dress, she called for Esther.

Esther returned to the room, then expertly fastened the bodice to the skirt with the straight pins.

"You never once poked me," Veronica marveled aloud.

"*Jah*, years of practice," Esther replied with a teasing twinkle in her eye.

Veronica looked about for a full-length mirror to evaluate her new look, but there was none. "Why isn't it a whole dress? I mean, why not stitch it together?"

"We make our own clothes, and it is easier to make a dress fit as the waist expands, for pregnancy or weight gain as we age, if it is not stitched together." Esther picked up a brush from the dresser. "Now, let's get your hair up."

A few moments later, Esther had twisted Veronica's tresses into a bun and secured a white bonnet on her head. "The prayer *kapp* makes your Amish look complete. The Bible tells us that a woman is to keep her head covered while she prays. And since we are always to be ready to pray, we wear it all the time. They also identify us with our church districts, since *kapp* styles vary from group to group."

"It shows that you belong." Her heart ached deep inside. How long had it been since she felt like she belonged…

anywhere? *With anyone?* Her mind raced through the past twenty years. She hadn't felt included and wanted since that fateful moment hiding in the clothing rack with her sisters. Being a part of that sister group had been the best part of her life. What would she give to be with them again?

Esther offered a sad smile as she spoke in a comforting tone. "Right now, you belong here. With me and Matthew." She lightly ran a hand down Veronica's arm.

Tears welled in her eyes despite her best efforts to keep them contained. They had been threatening to escape since yesterday's events, and she had managed to keep them at bay, until Esther drew her close into a hug.

That warm embrace was all it took.

Her composure crumbling, Veronica couldn't stop the release of what felt like gallons of tears she'd been holding on to for two decades. Of course, she'd cried at times over the years, but it had never been an emotional release. With someone she trusted. Never where she was comforted and consoled, and felt a measure of catharsis. She had longed for a friend but also had felt a huge distance from humanity for so long.

As the damp spot on the other woman's shoulder grew, a peacefulness and easiness with Esther settled over Veronica. Why? Was it her faith in God? Or maybe her life choices? Esther didn't seem to worry about anything. But could Veronica ever trust someone she couldn't see? That question would have to be answered another time.

Gradually, the tears dried and the hiccups were soothed. Veronica stepped back, staring at the wood floor.

"Are you ready for some breakfast? I made scrapple with some fresh bacon and biscuits." Esther ran her hand down Veronica's arm and led the way to the kitchen.

Breakfast was set out on pretty pink floral dishes on an

oilcloth covering the table. The kitchen opened to the living room, where more windows were covered with the same green shades. Plain white walls contained only a grandfather clock and another calendar, and an odd-looking floor lamp sprouted out of a table that covered a propane tank. That's what she thought it was, since it looked the same as the large bulbous containers men attached to their grills outside.

With Matthew nowhere in sight, she sat gingerly at the table, unaccustomed to being served. After a couple of bites of the fried slices of scrapple, she was ready to gobble up what remained on the serving platter.

"Do you like it?" Esther smiled from the sink, where she had plunged her hands into sudsy water.

She swallowed, not wanting to be rude and talk with food in her mouth, especially such a large bite. "It's fantastic. How do you make it?" Maybe she would have to add it to her repertoire of dishes.

"It's *wunderbaar-gut, jah*? It's super easy to make, but you have to start the evening before. It's just leftover ham or pork sausage with cornmeal and some spices. Put it in a loaf pan overnight. Then slice and pan fry in the morning." Her hands still in the sink, she nodded to a bottle of syrup on the table. "Some like to put maple syrup over it."

Veronica poured a little over a bite and quickly decided she needed it for the entire slice. As she sipped her second cup of coffee, her stomach satisfied, she forced herself to confront the fact that now that she was safe, at least relatively, she needed to call the phone number she had memorized twenty years ago when she first entered WITSEC. The phone number she was to use if she was ever in danger. But here she sat in an Amish home, and she had read that they don't use electricity. That would explain the odd lighting, powered by propane, as well as what had probably been batteries in the bedside lamp.

That would also make telephones a little tricky. A feeling of powerlessness snuck over her, and she rested her chin in her hand as she stared out the window. Now, what to do?

The door opened, startling her. She spun in her chair to see Matthew step inside and wash his hands at a separate sink in an outer entryway.

"All done with the chores?" Esther asked.

"*Jah*, it doesn't take long with so few animals. Dickens seems pleased to be back home after our trip." In the doorway, he stopped short when he spotted Veronica in the Amish dress and prayer *kapp*, staring as if mesmerized.

Veronica felt her cheeks grow warm as he continued to gaze upon her, and she pressed the back of her hand to her face.

Esther cleared her throat, forcing Matthew out of his stupor. Veronica glanced at his ister just in time to see her suppress a sly smile. "Are you okay, *mein bruder*?"

Matthew looked at her and then quickly turned his gaze back to Veronica. "*Jah.* I was just startled by how different our guest looks. It is a very *gut* disguise."

"I'm sorry to be a burden, and I appreciate all your help, but I need a telephone. Where can I find one?" As much as she enjoyed the attention from a handsome man, she couldn't stay here forever. Life had to move on.

"I can get you to one. Just let me hitch up the buggy." Matthew spun on his heel and disappeared out the door.

After thanking Esther profusely, Veronica went outside and stepped into the buggy. About a mile down the road, he pulled off to the side of a small plywood hut with a window in the door about the size of a telephone booth. "Multiple Amish families contribute to the upkeep of the phone shanty and the payment of the bill," Matthew explained. "Just put my name in the log book, and we'll take care of it."

"Thank you." She gingerly stepped inside, the woodsy smell of sawdust strong. As she dialed the number she had memorized two decades ago, she wondered if this would be the end of her need for protection.

On the third ring, a female voice answered. After a pause while the woman on the other end put her on hold to retrieve her information, she said that Veronica's deputy marshal had retired ten years ago. Since everything in her life had remained quiet and normal, the US Marshals Service had not yet assigned a new deputy to her case. "We'll send someone out as soon as a new handler is assigned to you," the robotic voice assured her. "Within two hours. Probably."

Veronica's heart raced as she heard the hesitation in the voice of the apathetic woman on the other end of the line. Could she trust this person? This office? It had been so long that everyone seemed different. How much did they really know about her situation?

But what else could she do? This was the only pathway to safety and security.

As Veronica stumbled to come up with a meeting place, Matthew leaned out the buggy window and suggested the library.

Yes, a public place for safety. Her heart calmed a bit at the wisdom of the suggestion. A few moments later, the arrangements made, she returned to the buggy.

"The library, *jah*?"

"Yes. Thank you for that suggestion. If you could drop me off, I'll be out of your way."

"*Nee*, I will stay with you until the deputy marshal arrives. I cannot leave until I know you are in good hands." He clicked to the horse, and the buggy jerked forward.

So this was it. In a couple of hours, she would be back in the hands of the Deputy US Marshal and given a new name, a new identity, new protection. Then she would be shuttled off to a new location.

Her stomach twisted within her. She would never see the Amish country of Bent Grass, Indiana, or Matthew Yoder again.

Matthew pressed his lips together, trying not to remember, not to wonder, but failing miserably. When he had first seen Veronica in the Amish dress, the vivid green fabric matching her eyes, she had seemed to be a completely different person. No longer quite so tough and independent, although he was sure she was still that on the inside. But her outer self was beautiful and vulnerable. She had been attractive before and he had wanted to protect her out of an obligation, but the dress added the beauty of modesty and femininity in a way that her jeans and sweatshirt never could. How anyone could want to hurt her he would never understand, and he didn't think that was just his Amish aversion to violence influencing him.

What if she didn't have to leave? To go to another location the government would assign to her? What if she could stay with him, safe in his company? In his arms?

He shook his head to get rid of the thoughts, slowly realizing Veronica was tugging at his arm.

"Matthew?"

Her gentle voice pulled him from his daydreams. He tightened his grip on the reins, grateful that the horse could steer himself when needed. *"Jah?"*

"Are you alright? You glazed over for a few minutes."

He turned to see her face crinkled with concern.

"I am fine." He swallowed. "Just thinking." He turned the horse right on the next road, heading for the library.

"So I was wondering…" Her voice faded away as if she was reluctant to say whatever would come next.

"*Jah?* Wondering what? You can ask. We Amish are used to all sorts of strange questions." Sometimes, it did seem that their lifestyle choices were quite different, but most of the time it just seemed as if the whole world had gone crazy. He glanced at her with a smile to sooth her anxiety. Whatever she wanted to know, he could take it.

"If you're sure…" She paused, then blurted out her question. "What happened to your leg?"

Matthew's hands involuntarily spasmed, making the reins jerk a bit. That was not the question he had expected. But it was out now, and since he most likely had no hope of a future with this beautiful woman after the US Marshal picked her up at the library, he might as well tell all, at least an abbreviated version of it. He sighed with resignation. "When I was twenty years old, a *haus* fire trapped *mein mamm* and *daed* inside. I rushed in to get them out, but the flames and the smoke were too much. I had to jump out of a second-floor window and broke my leg. I went to the hospital, but it didn't heal properly. So now that one is shorter than the other."

"What happened to your parents? Are they alright?"

A familiar wave of nausea swept over him, the bitter taste of bile rising in his throat. It happened every time he remembered the horrors of the fire. "They died in the fire."

"Oh, no." Veronica put her hand gently on his forearm. "I'm so sorry."

"It was a long time ago." Time had lessened the hurt a bit, but it had never disappeared completely.

"So now it's just you and your sister?"

"*Jah*, here in Bent Grass. We have extended family in Lancaster County." A tsunami of loneliness hit him with his admittance.

"But don't the Amish usually marry young? Does Esther have a boyfriend, or whatever you call it in the Amish community?" Veronica fingered the edges of her apron.

"*Nee*, although I think there are young men who would be interested in courting her if she wasn't so busy running a *haus* like adults have to do." If he could stop needing her help, she might have a chance at marrying and having a family of her own.

"What about you?" Her voice trembled on the last word.

"Me?" *Ach, Gott* help me, he prayed silently. "Well..." He cleared his throat, paused, then cleared it again.

"You don't have to tell me if you don't want to."

Was his hemming and hawing that obvious? "*Nee*, it's fine." He cleared his throat one last time. "At the time of the fire, I was courting a young *maedel*. I thought we were getting serious. But when my parents died and then I was permanently handicapped—plus I suddenly had a little *schwester* to raise—it was too much for her. The *maedel* ended it."

"That must have been painful, adding insult to injury like that."

"*Jah*. Literal injury." He tapped the knee of his disabled leg. There didn't seem to be any need to explain that there had not been a courtship since then. His disability demonstrated the reason enough.

"Maybe there'll be another girl."

Matthew appreciated her hopeful attitude. He would be an odd Amish man if he didn't want a family, but by community standards, he was an old, confirmed bachelor by now.

"*Nee*, I doubt it. All Amish *maedels* are married by my age, and I would not feel right marrying a girl of eighteen when I am in my thirties." He pushed away all the emotions that threatened to surface. Not only did he not want to show any to this stranger, but feelings would also serve no helpful purpose. "I'm fine as a bachelor. It does not seem to be *Gott*'s will that I marry. I accept that. It is what it is."

And yet, his brain whispered to him, he now had a new goal, one that *Gott* put right in his path at the bus station. This was his opportunity to prove to himself that he was a good protector, strong and able to make good decisions. This beautiful creature seated next to him in his buggy needed him. But then adrenaline spiked inside him with a new fear. What if he couldn't protect her? What if the worst happened and she was injured or killed because he failed? Then he would be an abject failure, no good for anyone or anything.

They rode in silence for a couple of miles, Veronica continuing to swivel about, checking for anyone following them. Matthew understood the necessity, considering her current situation. He watched in the side mirrors as well. But what a distressful way to live life. A silent prayer rose in his heart for her well-being.

The one-story redbrick building that housed the public library appeared down the road. A few minutes later, he parked in the space designated for buggies, marked by a hitching rail at the side of the building. No other buggies were there, but Matthew couldn't decide if that was good or bad. Could be good, as he wouldn't have to explain Veronica to anyone. But on the other hand, it could be *bad* since they couldn't blend in with other Amish. They would be obvious to all.

Inside, with Matthew in the lead, they moseyed through

the main areas looking for the contact. He stopped at the end of a book stack, browsing the titles, in an effort to be inconspicuous. When Veronica became interested in the movie section, he gently took her hand and wandered them toward the children's section in the back.

"The Amish don't watch movies," he murmured to her out of the corner of his mouth. "No electricity, remember?"

"*Jah*," she whispered back in her best Pennsylvania German accent. She grinned, her cheeks pink, and followed him through the library, continuing to hold his hand.

Despite their effort to find the US Marshal, no one seemed to notice them in any significant way, such as prolonged eye contact or head nods.

"When is he supposed to be here?" Matthew asked.

But Veronica only shrugged. "The woman on the phone couldn't say. And I don't know what he looks like. I guess he'll find us."

They continued to browse the books, trying to look casual but keeping their eyes and ears open. As Matthew scanned the Amish fiction section, wondering how accurate those stories actually were, a tall man in a uniform strode purposely into the main area of the library. He stopped near the middle, ran a hand over his dark hair and looked all around the space, but not at the books. With an expression that indicated he was trying not to look as intense as he actually felt, he scrutinized the people around the common area.

The hair on the back of Matthew's neck stood at attention, alarm bells clanging in his spirit. Something wasn't right. Slowly, he stepped in front of Veronica, nudging her to move into a place of concealment behind him and into the aisle.

"Do you see him?" he whispered.

Veronica's apple scent tickled his nose as she leaned closer in an attempt to see around him. "Yes. He's in uniform?"

"*Jah.* And I can't read the patch on his shirt to confirm that it says US Marshal."

"Well, that's suspicious. If I'm supposed to be in hiding, why would he announce his presence by wearing a uniform? Wouldn't that make me an obvious target?"

"Something doesn't add up." Matthew continued to conceal Veronica as he watched the man begin to move from aisle to aisle around the main area. Eventually, he would reach them if they stayed put.

"I agree." She reached her arm around him, pointing to the hair standing up on her arm, as if it was an alarm system.

Slowly, he stepped backward, urging her to do the same, while he kept his eyes on the man. A quick glance behind him revealed that the aisle ended in a set of study carrels with no way out. His heart began to beat in double time.

When he spun back to check on the man, his dark gaze crashed into Matthew's. They had been spotted.

The man ambled toward them, slowly but still with intent, clearly trying to act casual. He didn't identify himself but continued to move forward steadily.

There was no other way to go except for farther into the book stacks. At the end, they were pinned against the back wall in between a couple of empty study carrels.

"Veronica?" The man's voice hissed like a snake. She recoiled behind Matthew, fisting the back of his shirt.

"We need to see your identification." He tried for a bold, confident tone, unsure how it actually came out since he couldn't hear it over the clamorous whooshing in his ears.

An oily smile snaked across the stranger's face. Matthew felt Veronica shudder behind him. The man moved his hand as if he was going to reach in an inside pocket. Red flashed in his vision, a warning that something was terribly wrong.

Matthew stepped backward, nudging her farther away from the man, but they only hit the wall.

A moment later, the guy dodged around Matthew and lunged for Veronica. The air about him nearly crackled with malicious intent, as the uniformed man's odor of perspiration hammered Matthew while he struggled not to stagger backward. The man elbowed Matthew, shoving him away from Veronica and slamming him into the cement-block wall. His shoulder hit hard, pain stabbing through him.

"Veronica, *goh!*"

She immediately dropped to the floor and disappeared under the study carrel desk, leaving Matthew staring at the venom in the man's smile.

SEVEN

Veronica scurried away as quickly as she could on her hands and knees, climbing over chair stretchers and table supports, her heart pulsating somewhere in her throat.

If she could get away, maybe Matthew would be safe. The man didn't want him. Only her.

After crawling quickly under the connecting desks, she stood up on the other side. She risked a glance back and saw the man rush at Matthew. The interloper clearly hadn't calculated how solid and muscular Matthew was, and when the Amish man turned to the side at the last minute, their attacker rammed himself into Matthew's shoulder, but stumbled backward himself, into the study carrel. Veronica wasn't sure how that violence would mesh with Matthew's faith, but he had not been the instigator. In fact, all he had done was turn to the side. The imposter had committed all the violence. But this was no time for a religious or philosophical analysis. An overwhelmingly good feeling flooded her that Matthew had bought her a few seconds to get away while the man righted himself. All she could do was shoot up a prayer for her protector's own safety.

She ran to the end of the book stack but then stopped short when she saw how many people had piled into the library in the few minutes they had been detained down the aisle. Slowing to a walk, she glanced behind to see that Matthew had somehow gotten past the man and nearly caught up with her. With him just a few feet behind, she entered the common area. Winding through a line for the circulation desk, she saw a large family returning books in the chute, and a group of moms with young children headed for the children's department. On the other side of the large space, a bunch of people sat at a bank of computers. Veronica's pulse slowed slightly. Surely, the man, and Popov, if she was nearby, wouldn't strike out in the midst of a crowd.

"That man was not a US Marshal." Matthew's grumbling voice sounded right behind her as he caught up to walk at her side.

"No way," she agreed, turning to see him emerging from the book stack into the crowd. "And he's coming!"

Matthew grabbed her elbow and steered her into an aisle. "In here." He grabbed a random book from the shelf and instantly assumed a look as if he was reading.

"Good idea." Veronica pulled a large hardcover and opened it to hold it over her face just low enough that she could see over the top but high enough to cover the rest of her face. Should she remove the *kapp*? It probably identified her now, but removal would take too long with all the bobby pins and she'd still be wearing the dress. A woman's pink jacket on the back of a chair snagged her attention as something to cover her dress, but that would be stealing.

A couple of people squeezed behind them and continued down the aisle as the common area began to clear of the crowd. The gentle flashing of light as someone walked in front of a window drew her attention to the other side of the shelves. She peered over the tops of the books and through the shelving units, trying to identify what was making the hairs on her arm stand upright once again.

Were those his shoes a couple of aisles over? She had seen them up close just a few minutes ago as she crawled away. Nudging Matthew and making a low *ahem* sound, she squinted her eyes as she visually pointed through the shelves to the man's shoes. "That's him," she whispered. "Let's go."

There had to be a way to get to the side door and the buggy without running into the fake marshal. Veronica turned abruptly to lead Matthew away and clunked directly into a cart full of books. The force of her hip against the cart pushed it into the book stack.

A sheen of sweat slicked her forehead as she watched the stack wobble with the force of the impact. A couple of paperback books tumbled from the cart. A boy who couldn't have been any older than sixteen stood on the other side of the cart, staring at the shelves.

"Hey!" he protested loud enough for anyone in the vicinity to hear, a scowl spread across his face. But when he looked up and saw a couple of Amish folks staring at him, a look of chagrin reddened his complexion. Veronica put her finger to her lips to shush him. The kid looked around, his eyes wide. An older librarian at a nearby desk made eye contact with him, her eyebrows raised in a question. When he looked back to Veronica, she flashed him her most charming smile and mouthed, *Sorry.* The boy picked up the novels from the floor, never taking his eyes off Veronica.

She touched the back of her hand to her forehead. That could have been close, and as odd as it seemed, her smile had saved them. She didn't get out a lot, hiding in witness protection, and didn't have many relationships. Even though it felt dorky, she had practiced her smile in the mirror of her tiny apartment bathroom, just to be ready if she ever did meet someone. It definitely had come in handy just then, staving off a call for security or even the police.

But as she surveyed the common area, searching for clearance to get out, the imposter stepped out from a book stack across the space. His searching gaze slammed into Veronica. Without hesitation, he strode directly for them.

After grabbing the shelves with one hand for support, she elbowed Matthew and cut her eyes toward her attacker. His gaze widened as he spotted the man and nodded his reassurance to her. She nudged him to the right, and he quickly rounded the end of the aisle with Veronica on his heels. Hope surged in her that the shelves could hide them from view as she stepped around Matthew and pushed through the door to the children's department. Their saving grace was that the henchman was unlikely to accost them in a public place, where someone would alert the police.

Inside the kids' area, she led Matthew past a colorful book display and a bank of computers to more book stacks. Stuffed animals, block creations and growing plants populated the top of the short shelving units. Veronica slowed her hurried walk, Matthew following suit, and she peered between a large stuffed bunny and a castle built of interconnecting blocks. Had the man followed them into the children's department? Could he see them? She hunched over as she walked. Trying to be smaller. Less visible.

It was the story of her life.

The end of the aisle came much too quickly. She turned abruptly and stopped, Matthew bumping into her side as she nearly tumbled into a stack of what looked like reading pods. The ceiling-high structure, made of stacked, side-by-side spheres, provided semiprivate, quiet reading spaces.

An idea struck her. She grabbed a couple of large picture books from a cart, and handed one to Matthew. "Let's hide in these."

"*Gut* idea. If we need to, we can escape out the other side."

She nodded her agreement and climbed into a sphere a few feet off the floor. With only her shoulders inside, it became abundantly clear they were sized for children. Exhaling as much as she could, she squeezed in, muttering a prayer for safety. She quickly pulled off the *kapp* so she wouldn't look like she was waving a white flag of surrender.

As soon as she settled, cross-legged and hunched, Matthew removed his hat and held it inside the picture book then lifted his foot to the ledge to climb in behind her. As he tried to shove inside, his shoulder and upper arm pressed against Veronica. She tried to ignore his warmth but couldn't keep from noticing how muscular he was. It was only logical, she admonished herself, since he took care of animals every day and lifted heavy boxes of books running his store.

With one last effort, he put his foot back on the ground. "I don't think we'll both fit," he whispered.

Veronica felt a frown grow on her face. "No, I don't think so, either."

Her stomach clenched with sudden nausea. Surely, she would feel safer with him there next to her, protecting her. At least he would still be nearby.

But would that be enough?

Matthew spun around to check the children's department for any appearance of the man. Undoubtedly, the woman named Popov was also here somewhere.

He listened to Veronica's rapid breathing behind him,

easily able to hear it over the din of the *kinner* and their parents. Did she expect him to climb into another pod? That didn't seem right. It would be too far away. Instead, he stayed where he was, directly in front of Veronica's pod, protecting her while hiding in plain sight. He grabbed several more books to keep in a stack against his front while holding the large picture book open in front of his face and shoulders. Perhaps the pile of books would be big enough to hide his Amish shirt and suspenders. He shot forth a prayer for the strength and creativity to keep this beautiful woman safe.

"Veronica." Would his low whisper float up to her? "He's leaving."

In his peripheral vision, Matthew saw her stick her head out of her pod. He angled his head toward the windows opposite their hiding space and watched the man in the uniform, now with his jacket off, slide into a dark four-door sedan. Was that the Popov woman in the front seat? Matthew squinted but couldn't quite tell. Of course, he didn't know her face as well as Veronica's. But if that was Popov, then that was probably the man who had been with her at the bus station.

"I see." Her breath puffed on his cheek as she exhaled in relief.

"Is that the woman?"

"*Jah*, that's Nadia Popov."

Veronica's accent wasn't quite right, but Matthew couldn't tamp down the smile that sprang up at her attempt to use the Pennsylvania German language of the Amish. She was adorable.

"Stay there a few more minutes." He kept his voice low, partially out of habit and partially out of respect for the library. He shifted against the pods, making the entire structure shake. "Just to be safe."

"I still don't think I could recognize that man if I saw him again." Veronica fingered her *kapp*. "I was too busy trying to figure out where we could hide from him, and I only saw him for a brief moment."

"Just before we came through the door into here, I got a good look at his face. *Ach*, I could definitely recognize him again." Matthew tried not to grimace at the memory of the menace etched across the man's countenance.

Veronica exhaled slowly, like a pressure cooker that needed a release before it exploded. "I know this doesn't mean I'm safe and the whole thing is over." Relief sounded in her voice. "But I appreciate your determination that you could recognize the man again and that you'll see this all the way through. I won't ever forget your help." She patted him on the shoulder in what felt suddenly to Matthew like a patronizing gesture.

Her statement made it clear that she would be on her way as soon as she was out of danger. She had no further need for him than simple protection. Fine with him. With his handicap, he wasn't a candidate for a long-term relationship with anyone, anyway. He wouldn't be able to take care of a woman the way she wanted. *Nee*, needed. A woman wanted a big, strong man to carry heavy things and protect her and her *kinner*. That had been painfully proven the night his parents died in the fire because of his failure. Not only would he not be a good husband, but he also couldn't be a good father, either, if *Gott* should ever bless him with *boppli*.

Ach, he just needed to focus on the current goal and not fret about the future. Reminding himself for the thousandth time that tomorrow would worry about itself and his

Heavenly *Fater* already knew what he needed, he shifted his feet and tried to lean more comfortably against the pods.

"As long as they are there," Matthew said and nodded toward the sedan outside, "and we are able to watch them, let's stay put."

"Agreed."

He kept his eyes trained on the vehicle. Popov and the man just sat in the car, the man watching the front entrance of the library while Popov seemed to keep her attention focused on the side of the building as if waiting for an animal to emerge from its cage. For all practical purposes, that's what they were, Matthew begrudgingly admitted to himself. The library had back doors, of course, but they only led to an asphalt driveway that circled the building. On the other side of the driveway was a rock quarry—a huge hole in the ground surrounded by piles of stone no one could climb through.

His mind reeled with the effort of finding escape options, but he could think of none.

Nee, they were trapped like ducks waiting for the hunter.

A couple of Amish wandered by the pods with children in tow. They cast strange looks at Matthew, who obviously tried to shield his clothing with the books as Veronica held her *kapp* in her hands. But they simply nodded in greeting. He smiled a *hallo* and quickly rejected a thought that popped up. To ask them for help would mean putting these good folks in danger, and he refused to pull anyone else into their peril.

Tearing his gaze from the sedan for a moment to check on Veronica, he whispered, "It is *gut* to see more Amish arriving. That means there will be buggies out back. We may not be so noticeable when we leave."

He prayed that would be true. But as he returned his concentration to the car outside, the imposter suddenly leaned forward. His stare pierced Matthew's gaze as he made eye contact, a sneer snaking across his face.

They could hide no longer.

EIGHT

A tingle rippled across Veronica's skin, and she leaned out of her pod to look down at Matthew. His posture had stiffened, and she followed his line of sight out to the black sedan, where the man was staring menacingly at Matthew.

They'd been spotted. An adrenaline spike threw her into high-alert mode. It was time to move on. That's what life in the past two decades had taught her. Don't get comfortable. Don't settle in. Don't stay in one place too long. That last bit of wisdom applied to any length of time, even minutes.

Keep moving.

Without speaking, she slid from her reading pod and followed Matthew to exit the children's area, moving toward the side entrance, where the buggies were parked. He dropped his books on a cart but continued to carry his straw hat as if trying not to draw attention to himself. He did stand out from most other patrons, who were dressed in what Matthew would call *Englisch* clothing. Esther had told her that the hat was a valuable part of the male wardrobe, a symbol of his commitment to his Amish community. Now, though, he held it at his side, opposite the windows, as if trying to hide it, probably for their protection. As they walked as nonchalantly as possible toward the exit,

Veronica murmured another prayer for their safety, especially Matthew's.

At the side door, he raised his hand in a stop gesture. Veronica hung back, her heart beating a staccato rhythm. Matthew glanced backward, and she touched his shoulder to reassure him she was alright. Slowly, he pushed open the door and peeked out. On tiptoes to see over his broad shoulders, Veronica watched a buggy pull into a parking spot. She exhaled slowly, relieved that there would be some cover for their escape attempt. Would their attackers in the sedan be able to see them come out the door? She just couldn't tell from her angle.

As Matthew watched for the right moment to exit, she searched her spirit for an extra dose of courage. She could do this. No, she *had* to do this. They couldn't stay trapped like rats in a library maze. She straightened her shoulders and quickly pinned the *kapp* back into place.

The clip-clop of horse hooves on pavement grew louder as a buggy appeared around the side of the building.

Without taking his focus from the buggy, Matthew murmured, "Be ready to move."

This was it. She clutched his arm, a desperate move to leech some of his boundless strength. He glanced down at her hand on him, breaking his concentration on their escape. Her heart pounded at his expression. Was her touch inappropriate? She was unsure how the Amish world worked, but she couldn't force herself to let go. Anxiety coursed through her, and Matthew's strong presence was all she had to keep her upright and moving forward.

As the buggy drove past, Matthew whispered, "It's headed for a spot beyond ours."

She leaned forward to see as he grabbed Veronica's hand from his arm, planted it firmly in his own hand and pulled her out with him. With Matthew slightly in front, they walked behind the buggy, keeping pace with the slow and steady plodding of the horse. Hidden from view by the height of the Amish vehicle, they reached Matthew's buggy, and he helped her climb in. He let go of her hand to hurry around to his side before the other buggy passed them completely. Veronica instantly felt cold seep in between them at the absence of his touch, a shadow of loneliness descending upon her.

Matthew hopped in and grabbed the reins. "The car is still there."

"So you can see them?" Veronica craned her neck to look but couldn't see anything but the inside of the buggy. "That means they can see us, too."

"*Jah*, maybe. I can't quite tell if they saw us get in here or even realized who we are." He spun back to her. "If you get in the back seat and scrunch down, they'll only see me."

"Good point." She looked over his clothing, trying hard not to notice how handsome he was. "But your shirt is bright blue. They've surely noticed that. Maybe you should cover it up."

"*Jah*. Check under the back bench seat."

She clambered over the seat and lifted the cushion to reveal a storage area. "The only things in here are a couple of heavy gray blankets. You don't want one of those on a warm summer day."

"*Ach*, that's to use in the cold winter weather." He held out a hand to take it. "But if that is all we have, it'll do."

Veronica maintained her grip on the blanket. "Are you sure?"

Matthew turned and pulled the blanket out of her hands. "*Jah*, I'll do what is necessary to keep you safe." He tugged the dark gray blanket over his shoulders and arranged it until it covered his shirt completely.

"*Denki*," she whispered in her best Pennsylvania German accent.

She hauled the second blanket out of the storage compartment. Maybe the Amish kept two blankets in their buggies so each bench seat had one? It sounded cozy for snowy winter weather, but now?

Now, she slumped in the seat, staring at her shoes as weariness consumed her. She was tired of running. Of hiding. Of always having to look over her shoulder. But if she gave in to her fears, it would all be over. The End.

She couldn't let that happen, if only for Matthew. He seemed to feel enough guilt, enough inadequacy, already over the death of his parents. She couldn't let this turn into what he would perceive as another failure.

Swallowing down the thick lump in her throat, Veronica swung her feet up on the bench to lie down. Determination to get through just one more day swelled within her middle, and she tugged the blanket over her as Matthew pulled the buggy through the library parking lot.

She was hidden, and he was disguised. But would it be enough to escape detection?

It had taken some coaxing to get Dickens to back up and then turn in the opposite direction from the exit. The poor beast had been to the library so many times that Matthew typically didn't have to guide him at all. But now, going backward through the lot and out the entrance to avoid the sedan, seemed too much to ask of the animal.

Matthew couldn't do anything else but push forward, though. It seemed the test of his greatest fear had arrived.

If anything happened to someone else in his charge, he didn't know what he would do.

The clip-clop of the horse's hooves on the pavement didn't soothe him as it normally did. In fact, he barely heard it over the continuous whooshing in his ears. At least no buggy was trying to come in the entrance as he was trying to exit.

A whisper floated to him from the back seat. "Can you see them? Popov and the man?"

Tugging the blanket farther up on his shoulders with one hand, he glanced all around like his head was a spinning top. He didn't want to miss anything by not being vigilant enough. "*Nee*, but I cannot see the other side of the building."

At the road, a couple of buggies were approaching. With a wave that served as both a greeting and a request to pull onto the road, Matthew clicked to Dickens and lightly slapped the reins to move them out in between the two buggies. So far, his plan to blend in with the other Amish seemed to be working. He put his hat back on and held up his palm to say *denki* to the other driver.

A loud sniffling reached him from the back seat. "Are they gone?"

He checked all around one more time. "*Jah*, I think we have avoided them." *For now.* Surely, this was not the end of it, but he didn't say that aloud. "You can sit up." He checked both side mirrors and then turned enough to see her pull down the blanket and swipe a hand at her eyes. "Are you alright?"

"Physically, yes. But you can see why I have a hard time trusting, especially law enforcement. The US Marshals' office was supposed to send someone for me, and then Popov and that guy show up." She leaned against the side wall and closed her eyes as if trying to block out the world and all her troubles.

"I understand completely." Matthew glanced back, grateful that his horse knew to keep pace with the other buggies. "I was raised to be wary of law enforcement as well. The Amish church is our ultimate authority, and the police are too often intrusive. Those community attitudes are beginning to change, but it is difficult to throw off one's upbringing."

"*Intrusive?* They changed my entire life." Veronica's sniffling ended in a snort of derision.

"Does that mean you don't want to notify the police after seeing these two at the library?"

"Absolutely not. Besides, what would they say? Popov and her thug are gone. And we didn't get a license-plate number from their vehicle since Indiana doesn't require front plates." She paused. "There's nothing to tell them."

He glanced back to see that she had thrown off the blanket completely. A few strands of hair had escaped the *kapp*, and her beautiful reddish-blond hair shone in the sunshine. "*Jah*, I agree."

"I do need to call my real handler at some point, though. Can't live my life on the run." Her sigh mingled with the breeze coming through the side window.

An ache rose up in Matthew to sit next to her, to put an arm around her, to encourage her. Veronica had lived such a secluded life, hiding out and avoiding people. She'd been through so much heartache. So much trauma. But she'd come through it with a remarkable resilience that was truly unmatched.

She deserved to be safe. For this all to be over.

But when *would* it be over? Would *Gott* grant that to her?

He shook his head as if to rid his mind of unwelcome

thoughts. *Jah*, he had had his share of doubts about his faith. Hadn't everyone? They had grown particularly invasive in the months after his parents died. He had struggled through them, talking with the bishop on occasion. While he considered his faith to be solid now, his life had been gray and the same every day, which made it difficult to find joy and a reason to get out of bed in the morning.

Until Veronica.

The beautiful redhead had demonstrated to him that he had a *gut*, safe life. *Jah*, he missed his *mamm* and *daed*. But he had no real reason to complain. That was not the Amish way, anyway. But he had discovered what was missing.

Jah, a zest for life.

But primarily, companionship beyond a younger sister.

Maybe it was time to overcome the mental handicap that plagued him and realize that his physical disability did not limit him nearly as much as he thought. He scrubbed a hand across his face. Maybe he was capable of leading a family. It might even honor his parents if he had a wife and raised children in the Amish faith that his own parents had passed on to him.

Matthew turned back to Veronica. She remained low in the seat but was cognizant of her surroundings, ever vigilant.

No matter how attractive the woman was, this *Englischer* couldn't possibly be the one to help him raise children in the Amish faith. He may have had doubts once upon a time, but he wasn't leaving the church.

And for sure and for certain, he did not want to be shunned.

NINE

As the buggy traveled up the dirt lane to the house, Veronica perked up in the back seat. In the dusky twilight, Matthew and Esther's house, with the lamplight glowing in the windows, radiated a cozy invitation.

But as she looked around the yard, she saw danger lurking everywhere—in the darkness behind the barn, in the bushes, in the woods on the other side of the field. Who knew where that evil Nadia Popov or her unnamed accomplice may be hiding, ready to jump out and execute her, simply because she had identified Popov all those years ago. How long would this haunt her? Her entire life? Would she never have a normal life of husband and children?

Singleness had been thrust upon her by events out of her control. Living a secret life, how could she lie to a man and pretend that all was okay or, if she told all, bring danger to his doorstep? She couldn't have a marriage based on the falsehoods forced upon her as a teenager. And if she did confess the truth, then he would be living a lie as well.

She glanced at Matthew, noticing his strong jaw and piercing eyes that saw so much more than he let on. He deserved better than her. The Amish were so good, so wholesome and so *noble* that she could never be good enough for Matthew. A romantic relationship would sully his faith by her presence alone. And if she wasn't honest with him from the very beginning but maintained the deception? Well, she wasn't sure what would happen, but Matthew had spoken of the bishop with trepidation. *Nee*, as Matthew would say, it was better to be alone.

The buggy jerked to a stop at the back door, and Esther ran out to greet her. After Veronica stepped down and toward the house, Matthew drove on to the barn.

"Esther, what are you going to do with these?" She pointed to a crate of clean metal cans. An idea to rig an invisible alarm system pinged her brain.

"*Ach*, they go out to the barn." Frustration tinged her response. "I just haven't gotten them there yet."

"Would you mind if I use some of the cans? And do you have some fishing line as well?"

The woman looked at her quizzically. "*Jah*, but you *Englischers* have some *ferhoodled* ideas. *Ach*, I will not even ask what you are going to do with these things." She smiled as she pulled some clear line out of a cabinet and then turned to go into the house.

Veronica stepped back outside and then, keeping one eye on the property's perimeter, deftly set up her early detection system. She moved quickly in order to get into the warmth of the kerosene lamps and the comforting ticktock of the grandfather clock. The library had been a disappointing episode, and she was ready for some peace and quiet.

Inside, she washed at the second sink as Esther pulled a pan out of the honey oak cabinets. "Would you mind if I cook the meal?" Veronica had no idea what all ingredients the Amish might have on hand, but surely Esther would have some traditional staples. It had been several days since she'd been able to cook, and her creative side was itching for some play time.

Esther's breath caught as her smile grew. "*Jah*, if you'd like. I can help with whatever you need." Her hand flew to her throat. "I've never had an *Englischer* prepare a meal for me before, except at a restaurant."

"You can be my sous chef." Veronica smiled at the younger woman, pleased with her joyful response. "How about lasagna?"

"*Jah*, I've always wanted to try it." Esther retrieved a hand-cranked appliance from a nearby cabinet and plopped it onto the kitchen table.

"Wait a minute. You've never had lasagna, but you have a pasta-making machine?"

"We make and eat egg noodles a lot, like with chicken. We just don't typically have meals where the main course is pasta." Esther pulled ingredients out of cabinets. "I make egg noodles to sell at the general store and the farmer's market in the summer, so I have special permission from the bishop to have the machine."

"That sounds like fun." Veronica fiddled with the settings so she could make the larger noodles for lasagna, and then turned the crank to make it go. After a couple of rotations, she turned to Matthew's sister. "Why don't you continue this while I get started on the sauce?"

Esther took the handle while Veronica opened a jar of home-canned tomatoes and sprinkled spices into a pot. Soon, a wonderful garlic-and-bread aroma filled the house. "That smells *gut*!"

"I hope it tastes as good as it smells." She chopped a head of iceberg lettuce for a salad.

"I'm sure it will." Esther ran into the living room and returned a moment later with a couple of books. "I noticed that dish is just like this recipe." She dropped the newer book on the countertop and then flipped through the older cookbook until she stopped at a page titled Best Lasagna Ever.

With just a glance at the newer book written under her pen name Penelope Cupcake, Veronica laid down the knife when she spied the older, worn book splotched with stains. Her vision blurred with tears as she reached out to touch the cover gently. A nearby chair provided the seat she needed. She knew that book. Both books. Had several copies of her own back at her now-abandoned apartment. Her heart twisted violently within her chest as the loss came rushing back as fresh as the day it had all happened.

In her peripheral vision, she saw the younger Amish woman staring silently at her. Esther looked several times between Veronica and the old, stained book, and then she slowly turned it over as if that might explain Veronica's reaction.

The back cover displayed a large photo of the author and his family. With a trembling hand, Veronica pointed at the oldest of three girls in the photo.

"Do you know this cookbook? This family?" Esther asked gently.

Her finger moved to the woman in the photo. "My mother," Veronica whispered hoarsely. She pointed to the man. "My father. He was a famous chef and wrote this book."

Esther jabbed at the name of the author. "But your last name isn't—"

Veronica cut her off. "No. Don't say it." She couldn't bear to hear the name that had been hers when life was right and perfect, as it should be for a little girl. She moved her finger to point at the oldest girl again. "That's me." A large tear slid down her cheek and fell on the book with a splat. She held her breath to fight back the rest of the tears that threatened.

Esther examined her face with an intense look, as if the kind Amish woman was looking deep inside her soul. In that moment, Veronica made a decision. No more lies to this wonderful family. They deserved the truth.

"Yes, that is my real last name." She hiccupped back a few tears. "That is—was—my family." Pointing at the newer cookbook, she confessed, "And I'm Penelope Cupcake."

Gott, help!

Matthew rushed through the evening chores, thinking about the mysterious *Englischer* inside his house. He had already unharnessed Dickens and given him fresh hay and his evening meal, as well as tucked the buggy away into its slot. Now, his hand on the scoop down inside the barrel of dry cat food, he paused, remembering the scent of her strawberry-blond hair and the twinkle in her vivacious green eyes. If only he had a wife in his house, fixing his supper, rather than his *schwester*.

Ach, he was getting ahead of himself. He was as bad as an adolescent getting ready for his first singing.

He quickly filled the food and water dishes for the barn cats, stepping carefully around the kitties that tried to rub against his legs. Esther was *wunderbaar-gut*, and he would do anything for her. But at the end of the day, he wanted a wife who would welcome him home with a kiss. Would *Gott* ever grant him that blessing?

Leaning his head against the top board of the horse's stall, Matthew inhaled deeply the pungent scent of straw and horse flesh, and said a prayer that *Gott* would show him what to do and tell him what to say.

His tasks completed, he peeked out the barn door to check the yard and its perimeter before he crossed to the house. Adrenaline made his heart pound at the realization of how quickly that had become a habit. How had Veronica been able to stay sane and functional with a constant threat?

The yard and surrounding area looked clear, so he stepped out and closed the barn door behind him, heading toward home.

A pair of large oak trees framed the walkway about halfway between the barn and house. Matthew's stomach lurched at the sight of them. His *daed* had planted the twin trees for his *mamm* when they were first married. *Daed* had never been sentimental, so that was his way of promising a long life together. Matthew appreciated the thought, but his *daed*'s promise clearly hadn't worked out. He gently lifted his disabled leg over the root of one of the massive oaks, memories of the fire flickering around the edges of his mind.

As he walked between the trees, a loud clanging echoed around the yard. He jumped at the sound, a tremor running through him. *Ach*, what could that be? Hunching over to make himself smaller, he hurried toward the tree to hide himself as fast as his leg would allow. But with his third step, his ankle caught something, and the clanging ricocheted around the yard again. This time, his trembling lasted only a second. Was it an alarm of some kind?

At the oak, he examined the ground to find the source of the sound. A glint of the setting sun caught his attention, and he bent to run his finger along a bit of fishing line. With a gentle tug of his finger, the clanging started again, although a little quieter this time.

Veronica's face appeared in the window of the back door, Esther's smooshed in beside her. After darting her gaze all around the yard to look for danger, she spotted Matthew at the tree and smiled broadly at him, waving. She ran out of the house, Esther close behind.

Ach, it all became crystal clear. He had set off a perimeter warning signal that the ever-cautious Veronica had set up. Now that he could see it, he followed the nearly invisible fishing line as it skimmed about a foot above the ground, leading to the oak tree, running up its trunk, and ending in a handful of tin cans hanging from the lowest branches. When his ankle tripped the line, the cans, positioned up high, where they couldn't easily be seen, rattled together to make the loud, clanging sound that could apparently be heard even inside the house.

"What do you think?" Veronica's smile was infectious, and he couldn't help but smile in return even as he shook his head at her shenanigans. "I guess that was a good test of my early warning system."

"*Jah*, I thought it was *wunderbaar* clever." Esther examined the line as it led to the tree.

"*Ach*, you would, *mein schwester*. You loved to climb trees when you were younger." Matthew tilted his head at Veronica. "I would say it works."

She basked in his attention. "Well, I've developed many precautions over the… In the past. This one's primitive, but it'll do."

Matthew cocked his head, as if it could help him hear whatever it was she didn't want to say. She had cut herself off. Why? "Definitely," he replied. He looked at his *schwester*. "Supper ready?"

"*Jah*."

Matthew followed the *maedels* back to the house, unconsciously visually scanning the perimeter of the yard.

The table was set quickly, and the food arranged. "It

smells *wunderbaar*, like garlic and a sauce of tomatoes." He examined the pan. The Amish usually ate meals of meat with some sort of potato and both cooked and fresh vegetables. But this time there wasn't even a jar of home-preserved beets on the table, just a bowl of salad and a loaf of bread. "What is it?"

"Lasagna, *mein bruder*. Veronica made it." Esther held out the old cookbook for him to see the photo on the back. "She's a terrific cook. Her *daed* wrote this cookbook, and this is her family. Veronica wrote this newer one." Esther showed him a less stained cookbook. "She writes a cooking blog also."

The author's name was Penelope Cupcake. His gaze flew to Veronica as he realized a tiny part of her mystery had been revealed.

Veronica's face grew pink as she scooped a large helping onto his plate. The aroma wafted to him, and his stomach growled in response, making her smile. She served Esther and herself and then sat down on the bench, picked up her fork and scooped it into her lasagna. She paused with the utensil halfway to her mouth, and her eyes widened. Esther grinned awkwardly as Veronica lowered her fork, put her hands in her lap and bowed her head.

As usual, Matthew's thoughts wandered during the prayer. *Jah*, he was for sure and for certain thankful for the meal and for the one who prepared it. Maybe *too* thankful as his mind wandered into a daydream of having a wife sit at the opposite end of the table and several *bopplin* in between them.

A loud clanging from outside interrupted his thoughts. He jerked his head up to see both Veronica and Esther staring at him with wide eyes.

"We're all in here," Veronica whispered.

His *schwester* nodded her agreement.

"I will check." Matthew pushed himself up from the table onto his good leg.

The women rose to follow him. But even as he motioned for them to stay back, Veronica grabbed a cast-iron frying pan from a shelf and held it in front of herself like a shield.

At the door, he gingerly pulled back the light green curtain from the inset window and peered out into the yard. A moonless dark had descended on Bent Grass, and he could just barely see the outline of the big oak trees.

"I don't see anything." If Veronica wanted to call for law enforcement, there was no way to do it.

"Something has to be out there to trip the alarm. Shouldn't we find out what?" She reached around him to grab the doorknob, the homey and comforting scents of spices wafting around him.

"I'll get a flashlight." Matthew turned away and grabbed a large flashlight from a shelf on the inside porch.

As he turned back to shine the light out to the trees, Veronica opened the door. "*Nee*, wait!"

A split second later, something flew through the door and lodged in the wood trim around the entrance into the kitchen. A dart? Before Matthew could get in front of her to shield her, Veronica raised the frying pan once again, still staring into the darkness.

A second projectile flew through the door with a whizzing sound.

Veronica fell to the ground with a heavy thump.

A panicky bile filling his throat, Matthew sank to the floor next to her. *Gott, help!*

TEN

Sharp pain pierced her, then radiated throughout her chest, and Veronica fluttered her eyelids. She could see only the linoleum floor of the back porch.

A thousand different worst-case scenarios attacked her brain. She squinched her eyes shut in a desperate attempt to block some of the overwhelming stimuli. Maybe that would help get her focus back. But her mind had distilled her thoughts down to one still image from twenty years before: Nadia Popov with the tranquilizers she had used to kidnap children. That had been her MO. If a child resisted, Popov would stab her with a tranquilizer dart.

She couldn't just lie there and give up. She was stronger than that. Forcing her eyes open, Veronica saw the dart on the floor next to her. That meant Popov had graduated to a tranquilizer gun. Whether the intention was to kidnap her or make the drug so strong that it would kill her, Veronica wasn't sure. But she couldn't allow either to happen.

Fortunately, if the dart was lying on the ground next to her, that meant it wasn't stuck in her. The frying pan had also hit the floor, and her hand was still wrapped around the handle.

"Veronica! Are you hurt?" On his knees, Matthew slid to Veronica and laid a warm hand on her shoulder.

She rolled over to gaze into his dark brown eyes, fine lines of anxiety crinkling the edges. "I'm alright."

"Can you stand?" He grabbed her hand to provide an anchor so she could pull herself up. "We need to get out of here."

As she reached an upright position, another dart whizzed through the door. It slammed into the woodwork next to Veronica, and she stared at its feathered end directly at the level of her chest. She swallowed hard, relieved that Popov, or maybe it was the man who had attacked them before, was not a good shot.

"Get the door closed," she instructed Matthew.

But as he reached for the knob, Esther screeched from the kitchen, "*Watch out!*"

An unseen force flung open the door, hitting Matthew into the wall behind with a loud thump. The slight form of a person dressed all in black rushed her and thrust sweaty hands on Veronica's arm, driving her backward. Veronica leaned forward and shoved back, her arms straining against her attacker. Trembling with the effort, the woman slowly raised a fist.

A tranquilizer dart was aimed straight at Veronica's heart.

Suddenly, a force from the side flashed through her peripheral vision. Right shoulder first, and grunting from the effort, Matthew pushed from his good leg to knock Popov off balance and away from Veronica. But the reprieve was short-lived.

A split second later, her attacker had regained her footing, and was preparing to strike again. Fist raised, the woman rushed Veronica, the tranquilizer dart in her hand. A surgical mask covered most of her face, but her eyes fixated on Veronica's heart.

"Go," she grunted at Matthew as she strained against the dart aimed at her chest. "Get Esther. Go."

His sister whimpered as she rushed toward the door. But Matthew hesitated. Was he being noble, thinking he should protect her, despite the community's policy of no violence? But his faith should not suffer because of her. No, the best thing would be for him to escape.

"Matthew," Esther urged. "Let's get the buggy ready."

"Go!" Veronica gripped the assailant's wrist and slowly pulled the dart away from her own heart.

When Matthew saw that she had the upper hand, he finally exited with Esther to ready their getaway.

But her foe only grew in strength. It seemed that evil knew no bounds, no restrictions, in the effort to overtake the innocent. The woman again thrust downward to stab Veronica with the tranquilizer dart. The heart-piercing needle-like tip of the dart wobbled back and forth as she struggled to get the attacker off her.

Sweat broke out on her brow with the effort as Veronica twisted loose from the woman's grip. Inhaling a deep breath, Veronica lunged for the frying pan, which had fallen on the other side of the porch. But the toe of her shoe caught on something, and she tumbled to the floor, sliding on her knees the rest of the way. Stretching, she wrapped her fingers around the pan. She slowly got to her feet, exhaustion beginning to set in, and raised it.

With the weapon poised above her, she paused. Should she do this? The Amish never allowed violence. They didn't join the military or learn martial arts or fight back if attacked.

But if Veronica *didn't* do this, she would be killed.

There was no choice.

As the attacker spun to face her, Veronica struck the side

of the woman's head. She tried to hit gently, but it *was* a frying pan. It would be a hard blow no matter how she managed it. Her assailant crumpled to the linoleum. Veronica stood still for a moment, drawing in deep ragged breaths, and watched the perpetrator's form for movement. With the toe of her shoe, she gently tapped the woman's foot.

No response.

With tears dripping down her cheeks and a thick lump in her throat, Veronica continued to clutch the frying pan in one hand. She kneeled down, and with her free hand put two fingers to the woman's neck. A steady pulse thrummed under her touch. *She was alive.* Veronica pressed her hand to her chest as if that would calm the thumping of her heart, then pulled away the surgical mask her assailant wore.

Now, there was no doubt. Veronica's attacker was, in fact, Nadia Popov, the kidnapper that she had testified against twenty years ago.

But where was the man? Her coconspirator?

A low moan filled the small back porch. Veronica's heart leaped in her chest as she saw Popov's arms move.

Now what? Did she have the mental strength to use the frying pan again if needed?

Gripping the reins so tightly his fingers hurt, Matthew leaned forward on the front seat of the buggy. He had pulled up as close to the door as possible, ready for a quick getaway. But no sound came from the back porch, and he wasn't sure what that meant. Had Veronica subdued her attacker? Or was Veronica the one who had succumbed to the violence?

"What do we do, *mein bruder*?" Esther perched on the front seat next to him, poised and ready to fly into action.

Although what that might be for a petite Amish woman, he couldn't fathom. "Shall I go see if I can be of help?"

He paused. He felt no guilt for his shove to Veronica's attacker. It had, in fact, only been slightly stronger than he might have used with Dickens, their horse, to get him into his stall. Veronica had been under siege, and Matthew hadn't even thought twice about helping her.

"*Mein bruder?* I can sneak to the door and get Veronica, *jah*?"

Esther's prodding of his arm brought him out of his reverie. "*Ach, jah.* But stay out of sight as much as you can."

Darkness covered the face of the land, and for safety, Matthew had not turned on the battery-operated lanterns on either side of the front of the buggy. He stared into the blackness, barely able to make out Esther's form as she crept toward the back door.

A few moments later, before he had time to utter much of a prayer to *Gott* for safety for all of them, Esther returned with Veronica jogging behind her. He released a huge breath.

Without Matthew telling her to, Veronica scrambled into the back and lied down on the seat, out of sight of any car that might pass them. Esther jumped up on the front seat next to him. With a nod from his sister, Matthew tapped the reins and Dickens began to pull them away from the house.

A thrashing from the woods on the other side of the yard disturbed the silence of the night. Matthew leaned out his side to see a man appear out of the trees, yelling words Matthew had seldom heard. Moving shockingly fast, the guy rushed for the buggy.

A gunshot exploded in the dark, narrowly missing the buggy and lodging into the side of the house.

Setting his jaw, Matthew faced forward and flicked the

reins again, desperate to get away before the assailant actually hit one of them. The horse lurched into a trot, a speed no human could keep up with. Matthew scanned the road as they pulled out of the lane, but no cars were visible. Apparently, Nadia Popov and her conspirator had parked their vehicle someplace where they couldn't jump in and give chase.

At least momentarily.

"Did we get away from them?" Veronica asked from the back seat, her voice muffled.

"*Jah*," Esther whispered.

"But stay down a bit longer, just in case." Matthew turned to look back at the house. "He's going inside now, probably for the woman."

"Inside?" Esther's voice trembled. "*Ach*, inside our home?"

"*Jah*, probably to get his partner in crime." His *schwester* most likely was concerned with the evil strangers rifling through their things or tearing up their home. But that wasn't likely.

A chill coursed down his spine as he urged the horse forward. Their car couldn't be too far away, and their target was Veronica.

ELEVEN

A sudden flash of lightning illuminated the night around them as a crack of thunder tore open the sky. The darkness intensified when the rain began, large drops plunking on the buggy roof in increasing speed.

After Matthew reassured her that no one had followed them, Veronica slowly sat up in the back seat and peered out the tiny rear window. How could he tell in such pervasive gloom? She ran a hand through her hair to straighten it after the blanket had ruffled it. Somehow, she needed to contact someone reliable at the US Marshals' office. This couldn't go on. She couldn't live her life on the run, and she certainly couldn't expect to be taken care of by Matthew and Esther indefinitely. Despite how much she enjoyed their homey lives, their freedom from anxiety and their simplicity of living, she had imposed on them long enough.

"Where can I use a telephone? I think it's time to call the police."

"*Ach*, are you sure?" Matthew checked out the side of the buggy again.

Veronica peeked out also, but blackness enveloped them. "Yes. If the US Marshals' office can catch Popov and her thug, it'll be all over, and I'll be safe. But I can't seem to contact anyone who will help me."

"At the very least, Matthew," Esther said as she touched his arm, "we need to make sure those villains get out of our home and the *haus* is secure."

"*Jah*, I agree with you *maedels*." He nodded at her over his shoulder before returning his attention to Veronica. "I just want to be sure you two are sure."

"Definitely. Then you can be rid of me." Veronica's voice sounded as hollow as her heart felt.

Matthew seemed to sag in the front seat, even though this was his opportunity to hand her over to someone else for babysitting. She was grateful for his willingness to keep going, but it didn't make sense that he would want to keep around an *Englischer*, as he called her, especially one who brought danger to him. That was the last thing she wanted. But whatever his reasons, she was grateful to have his protective services as well as his strength and comfort a while longer. Life would be as dark and gloomy as the outside when they had to part ways.

He sighed. *"Jah."* He exchanged another glance with his sister, but Veronica couldn't tell what they were both thinking. "There is a telephone shanty down the road. But I am afraid that if we stop there, so close to the *haus*, we risk being found."

In the rainy darkness, Veronica had no clue where they were or how far they had come, but she had no doubt Matthew knew. "Okay, yeah, we don't want to be nearby when Popov recovers." If the criminals were anywhere close, the chase would ensue all over again, and she had left her frying pan at the house. "So what's plan B?"

"I think it's best if we go to my bookstore."

"Plan B for bookstore. Sounds like a good idea." Veronica leaned back and hugged herself.

Peering out the tiny window in the back of the buggy,

she couldn't tell if anyone was behind them. If the bad guys *did* come after them, would they turn on their headlights? They would need the light to see the road, wouldn't they? Or perhaps they would elect to keep them off so they could sneak up on them… She rubbed a palm against her forehead. Her brain just didn't work like a villain's.

Spinning around to face front, she tried to focus on what should have been the soothing sound of rain hitting the buggy roof. She certainly had come a long way in just a couple of days. Was she more safe now than she had been when the supposed pizza delivery guy had knocked on her apartment door? She thought for a moment, listening to the pitter-patter of the raindrops. Yes, she was. No doubt. All because she had Matthew with her.

The horse—Matthew had called him Dickens, for the British author—tossed his head and rain flew from his mane.

Veronica propped her elbows on the back of the front seat, in between Matthew and Esther. "Will the horse be alright in the rain? He looks wet and miserable."

Matthew pulled on the reins, and the horse turned to the right, onto another country road. "*Jah*, he is fine." He turned to Esther with an eye roll. "The *maedel* is *ferhoodled*."

"*Ferhoodled?*" She tried to get the Pennsylvania German accent, but it didn't sound like when Matthew had said it. "Esther called me that, too. What does it mean?" Whatever he had said, it had made Matthew smile. It looked so nice on his face as Veronica stared at his profile that he could say that again, whatever it was.

"*Jah*, it means you are confused."

Okay, maybe she didn't want him to say that again. "How so?"

"You feel sorry for the horse, but it is an animal made

by *Gott* for work. So he is working. We will take good care of Dickens when we reach my bookstore, but for now, we need him to pull the buggy. That is his job, and it is *gut* for him to stay active."

"Is he safe on the road in the dark?"

"It is true the Amish do not travel much after dark. But there are not many cars out in this weather, which makes the roads safer for horse-and-buggy traffic. And we are almost there." He pulled on the reins again, and Dickens turned left.

As the horse continued to trot, pulling them ever closer to the bookstore and the call to law enforcement, Veronica clutched the back seat. Soon, her time with Matthew and his strong, comforting presence would come to an end.

She would be alone. Again.

Matthew wanted to knock his hand against his ear as if that could rid him of the sound of a car engine drawing closer. Goose bumps stood up on his arms. The noise was not in his imagination.

The revving slowly grew louder than the clip-clop of the horse hooves on the pavement.

If he could, he'd kick himself. Just as soon as he'd told Veronica that it was safe and there weren't many cars, here came one down the road. Driving rather quickly, too, judging by the sound. Maybe he should have turned on the lights on the buggy. Powered by a cordless tool battery that could last up to three hours, the lights were controlled by a console at the front of the buggy, at Matthew's fingertips.

What if that was a police cruiser approaching? He didn't want to get a ticket for not having his lights on in the dark as required by a new county ordinance. Or maybe it was just a vehicle trying to get somewhere in the dark? He definitely didn't want an accident. He flipped of a few switches, turning on his headlights and taillights as well as lights along the side, where a running board would be. He left off the interior light because, although he wanted to be sure the buggy was seen and carefully avoided, he didn't want anyone outside to be able to tell who was inside.

Most *Englischers* thought the Amish buggies were still like those from prairie days. Because the transportation was horse-drawn, it never occurred to them that the Amish might desire more safety as well as a few comforts with some style thrown in as well.

"*Ach, mein bruder,*" Esther whispered, "the lights? Are you sure?"

"*Jah.* A vehicle is approaching. They will see us with the slow-moving-vehicle triangle on the back. But this is for additional safety." *Or was it?* What if it was that woman and man, back to finish the job?

Veronica popped forward from the back seat. "Do you hear that?" The revving sounded closer.

"*Jah.*" Matthew's mind spun with possible options. He didn't want to discuss them aloud and worry the *maedels*. But he thought they were still a couple of miles from his bookstore. That meant that Twin Pines Road was just up ahead to the right. He doubted he could get there before the car caught up with them, and even if he did make it there, the road was wide enough for an *Englischer*'s vehicle. It wouldn't protect them.

Rain continued to pelt the windshield as he mulled over options that would hide Veronica from whoever was coming. That was the priority. And safeguarding Esther, Dickens and the buggy as well. It startled him that his primary thought was Veronica and not the *schwester* he had been looking after for years. Was that how much he had grown to care for Veronica over the past couple of days?

The car-engine noise sounded at the bumper now.

A split second later, the buggy jerked forward. Esther threw out her hands to catch herself on the console. "What was that?"

The impact pushed Veronica into the back of the front seat. After righting herself, she spun around. "There's a car back here, bumping us. It looks like it's on purpose."

"Get down, Veronica!" he admonished her. "We can't let them see you."

The car hit the buggy's bumper again. Matthew smashed his foot to the brake pedal to keep the buggy from bumping into the back of the horse. They wouldn't get anywhere if Dickens was injured.

"Matthew." Esther turned to him with panic in her eyes. "The lane to the old mill. Can we hide in there?"

His brain lit up with a mental map of the area. *"Jah."* It was a *wunderbaar* idea.

The buggy jolted a third time as the car struck it from behind. He hit the switch on the console to turn out the buggy lights. That could be a disastrous decision, but he prayed it would be a definite help. They had only a couple hundred feet to the turn.

"Can we make it?" Esther asked.

"Make it where?" Veronica's head lifted just above the back of the seat.

"A mill near here closed down a while ago. Farming in the northern Indiana Amish communities has decreased over the years, as everyone's taken factory jobs. The mill was deserted for quite some time, and trees and bushes have been reclaiming the lane leading to it. *Mein schwester* believes we could hide in that overgrown dirt road." Matthew gripped the reins in anticipation of the sudden turn.

Veronica made a sound of agreement that morphed into a squeal. "The car is back." She dropped below the seat to where Matthew couldn't see her.

Esther gripped the edge of the console. As the buggy lurched forward under the force of the impact, Dickens snorting his disapproval, Matthew turned him into the lane.

Instantly, branches filled with wet leaves slapped the storm shield. Rain continued to pelt the buggy as it dipped and swayed with the ruts of the lane. Matthew saw Esther's fingernails turn white with the effort of clutching the console to keep from being knocked about the inside of the buggy.

An Amish buggy wasn't built for off-roading. Was there another way?

He grasped the reins and searched the darkness for the road as the question rose in the forefront of his mind.

Did he really think he had the ability to keep his people safe?

TWELVE

Veronica squelched a screech threatening to erupt. As the buggy lurched down the lane, she gripped the edge of the seat to keep herself upright so she could peek out the front.

Matthew flicked the reins to keep Dickens moving. Damp, stray leaves broke off and worked their way into the buggy through the small opening between the storm shield and the side windows. One slapped her in the face, and she peeled it off then wiped the back of her hand across the wetness it left behind. They weren't tears, at least, but there was no telling how soon those might come.

The sound of branches scratching the fiberglass sides of the buggy made her cringe. Surely, that was damaging the vehicle, but it seemed Matthew had decided their safety came first. They could worry about the look of his ride later.

Even though all she wanted was to be safe in Matthew's strong arms— *Wait. Where did* that *come from?* She shook her head, as if she could shake out the wayward thought, then forced herself to check out the back window. "They aren't following."

He let the horse slow a bit and turned to peer out the back. A flash of lightning revealed the dark sedan still on the road, blocking the entrance to the lane.

Even if he could turn around in the narrow path, there was no exiting at that end. Not with the car there.

Neither of them had moved in their game of chicken.

But then, as more lightning streaked across the sky with an accompanying rumble of thunder, she breathed a sigh of relief as the car finally drove away.

"They don't want their vehicle to get marked by the scratching of the branches. Then it could be identified. Or get stuck in the mud and then they couldn't get away," Matthew mused. "But I have no doubt they will find us again."

"Find *me*, you mean." She slumped against the back seat and took a breath so deep it pained her lungs. "I've bothered you two long enough. I'm not your burden. Drop me off at the mill, and I'll find a phone on my own. When Nadia Popov sees that I'm not with you, she'll leave you alone."

An eerie structure loomed up on the right side. Matthew directed Dickens to pull the buggy over and stop. Darkness permeated the inside of the carriage except for what little illumination filtered in from the running lights. Large drops of rain plunked on the roof. It could be cozy, if there wasn't a killer after them.

The buggy lurched to a stop behind the horse. Good. They were going to let her out. A pang stabbed her chest. It wasn't *really* good, though, was it? Would she ever see Matthew again?

Veronica pushed gently on the back of the front seat, a nudge to get someone to get out to unlock the rear door for her. The closing mechanism only worked from the outside. She could climb over the front seat but didn't want to do that to Matthew and Esther.

Still, they didn't move.

Both turned to the back seat, Matthew putting his arm

across the top to pull himself around to look Veronica in the eye. "You are right about one thing."

"Fine." She nudged them again. "Whatever it is, I agree. Just let me out." The inevitable tears choked her throat, and she coughed to keep them at bay.

"You are right that they aren't following us. But the rest is hogwash. You are *ferhoodled* if you think we are going to drop you at the mill and leave you there to fend for yourself." His gentle brown eyes penetrated her soul with a warmth that caught her off guard. In her years of hiding, her relationships with others had been superficial out of concern for her own safety. This level of care unsettled her with its unfamiliarity, and she shifted on her seat. "I am going to do all I can to keep you safe until this is resolved."

Esther nodded her agreement, apparently not catching her brother's use of the word *I*.

Finally, a tear leaked out, and another, uncontrolled. "I'm scared."

He nodded his understanding and offered a deep sigh. "*Jah*. So now, we need a phone to call the police. I pray they will help us." A look of doubt flitted across his face. "It is only a couple of miles to *mein* bookstore."

"It won't be long now." Esther reached over the seat and patted Veronica's hand with her warm one.

Sure, just like the Amish woman said, it wouldn't be long. Veronica swiped her hand across her cheek to catch the tears. It wouldn't be long until Popov or her henchman got her.

It really would be all over when she was dead.

Short of telling Veronica that he was falling in love with her, how could he get her to believe that he was not leaving her in her distress?

Matthew scrubbed a hand across his chin. Now, he was the *ferhoodled* one. *Falling in love with her?* He needed to push that thought out of his head right away. No way would she want to be with him, an Amish man committed to his faith and his way of life, as well as a man with a disability that prevented him from taking care of her. No, he would be alone for his life. And he could accept that as long as it was *Gott*'s will.

Maybe.

He clicked to Dickens and tapped the reins for the horse to pull on forward down the lane. The wet, tired beast slowly moved into a walk. Matthew's heart went out to the animal. He had always admired the workhorse's ability to plod on through rain, wind and snow. As he mentally calculated how much farther until he could get shelter and fresh hay for Dickens, he prayed he would have the same level of stamina in protecting Veronica.

Several minutes later, the abandoned mill loomed large, a desolate structure that made Matthew's heart ache. It was always sad when an Amish-run business had to fold because it could no longer compete with the modern ways of the *Englischers*.

He nudged Dickens to continue on and soon turned the buggy onto the country road on the opposite side of the mill from where they had entered. But would this road be safe?

How well did those two, the woman Veronica called Popov and her accomplice, know the area? The rainy darkness surely worked in their favor, in addition to his detailed knowledge of the intricacies of the roads in Bent Grass. But was that an advantage? *Englischers* had their fancy phones that could show elaborate maps for wherever they were.

A church district a couple of counties away allowed GPS

on cell phones in buggies, but they were a bit more progressive and rather unusual for the area. Matthew was simply glad he was allowed a storm front, or as the *Englisch* liked to call it, a *windshield*, on his enclosed buggy. Some of the Old Order Amish didn't even allow that protection, and expected their members to travel in the snow and rain and cold in an open buggy.

Did Popov have GPS? A chill coursed down his spine. Still, though, Matthew figured his brain was better than any electronic device.

Please, Gott, *let it be so.*

They plodded on, the swaying of the buggy, the gentle thumping of the horse's hooves on the asphalt and the plunking of the rain on the roof a welcome, soothing lullaby. The precipitation brought a bit of a chill with it, and he turned up the propane-powered heater. Soon, he could see in his peripheral vision that Veronica sagged with tiredness in the back seat.

About a half mile down the road, vehicle headlights lit up the woods on either side from behind the buggy. Matthew's heart stuttered a few beats. *Ach*, not again.

Veronica jerked upright, her profile blocking the light coming in the little window in the back of the buggy. "Who is it?" A tremor could be detected in her voice.

"Hard to tell just yet. But they are coming fast." Matthew had never been one to sugarcoat a situation, and he wasn't about to start now. It wouldn't help Veronica in the least to downplay the seriousness of what they were facing.

The car swerved to the other lane, its tires squealing on the wet asphalt. Speeding up, the sedan pulled alongside the buggy, making the horse whinny and toss his head with anxiety. Just as Matthew pulled back on the reins to slow down Dickens and let the car pass, hoping to calm the animal, the passenger side window lowered. Matthew recognized the man who leaned his upper body out the window and grabbed the reins close to the bridle.

Esther clutched at his arm, and he sneaked a glance to find her eyes wide with fear. But Veronica reached over the back seat to pull his *schwester*'s hand away. "Let him drive, Esther. He looks like he knows what he's doing."

Esther withdrew her grip and hugged herself instead. "*Jah*, he does. I am just worried."

"*Denki*, Veronica." He nodded his thanks but didn't take his eyes off the road.

Matthew turned to the man in the car, their eyes meeting. A cold bolt coursed through him at the look of malice in the man's expression. The sooner he could get Veronica away from this evil, the better.

Who was this guy's target now, anyway? His behavior would either spook the horse and cause Dickens to run wild and injure everyone in the buggy, or he could force Dickens to stop, which would mean that the passengers couldn't escape. At the very least, a getaway wouldn't be easy in the dark pouring rain.

Different scenarios ran through his mind. None of them presented a good option—one in which they were safe and the bad guys were apprehended. Of course, he could just stop. But if the man's grip held tight enough on the reins, it could hurt the horse if Matthew forced him into a sudden stop, and he wasn't willing to do anything that could hurt Dickens.

With a loud grating noise, the vehicle's engine revved so close that his horse shook his head. The car slowed as the man seemed to tighten his hold on the reins.

Suddenly, he saw the thug reach into the inside of his

jacket, a glint of something metal flashing in the buggy's running lights. Did they mean to stop the buggy? But then what?

Whatever it was, Matthew couldn't let it happen. He must protect Veronica at any cost.

THIRTEEN

She could end this entire terrible episode of Matthew's life right now.

"If I disappear, he'll leave you two alone." Veronica pulled the gray woolen blanket from the back seat and yanked it over her head to hide her reddish-blond hair and green dress. She couldn't get out the rear door since it was locked from the outside. With a push off the seat, she propelled herself forward and tumbled headfirst over the back of the front seat. Esther quickly scooted out of the way.

"*Nee*, Veronica!" Matthew spun quickly to make eye contact, then returned his attention to the road. "You do not know the area. It is dark and raining. What if you get lost?"

She paused for a moment. Poor Matthew probably felt paralyzed with the villain holding his horse's reins on one side and Veronica trying to escape the buggy on the other side. She appreciated his protectiveness even though she didn't understand it. Sometimes he looked at her in a way that made her wonder if he was developing feelings for her, but then the sheer hopelessness of her situation hit her hard, knocking that notion out of her head. No one had cared about her since her parents were murdered. She wouldn't know what that felt like, anyway.

She had to get out of the buggy for Matthew's sake,

though. Tough to admit, but she was falling for him. And for him, that would be treacherous. As she glanced at the car driving alongside the buggy, it was clear that danger already had come for Matthew. She couldn't expect him to commit to a relationship under these circumstances. Neither could she tell him the truth of her life. *Her lie.* Once he knew everything, he, too, would be living that lie. She could never in a million years be good enough for him. She would sully his faith and his Amish heritage by her presence alone. What did they call it in crime novels? Guilt by association.

She wouldn't do that to the man who had captured her heart.

A snarl echoed through the rain. Veronica turned to see the man glaring at her, reaching for something in his coat she couldn't see. Lightning streaked across the night sky, revealing the steely glint of his eyes as they met hers. Her pulse sped into overdrive at the maliciousness emanating from him.

"You're done, girl." His voice sounded like tires on gravel.

Veronica fought to suppress a shudder, but a tremor around her shoulders still escaped.

Words no one should ever use or hear spewed forth from him as he raised a gun from his side. At least they were garbled by the rain.

Esther screamed, the sound tearing through the downpour. Matthew gripped the reins, unable to do anything to halt the disastrous situation. Veronica didn't know the first thing about driving a horse pulling a buggy, but she could see that Matthew could never reach the bridle to pry off the man's hands. He couldn't stop Dickens or he would risk injuring the horse if the man didn't let go. Nor could he speed Dickens up without the same danger of injury to his animal.

Veronica stole a deep breath. She must get out of there to save Matthew and Esther.

But she was too late.

Matthew suddenly jolted toward her, still clutching the reins, and threw himself in front of her. His weight pushed her to the side and into Esther's lap as a shot rang out.

Esther screamed again. Veronica grasped the back of the other woman's head and pulled her down.

Blood splattered the windshield as Matthew cried out in pain.

The buggy careened to the right, the car keeping pace. Veronica eyed the door and the latch to open it. Now was her chance. She turned as much as possible to see Matthew still sitting upright, grasping the reins with his left hand while holding his right hand over his left bicep. Blood seeped between his fingers. He had been hit, but the wound wasn't gushing. Good. From what she had read about injuries and first aid in her copious free time in WITSEC, it was probably a flesh wound. It would be painful but could heal without difficulty. If she ditched the buggy and drew Popov and her henchman away from Matthew, he would be free to seek the medical care he needed.

Reaching past Esther, Veronica grasped the door handle. Esther, eyes wide in her pale face, shook her head and grabbed Veronica's arm to pull her back. But the slender young woman was no match for her, and Veronica peeled off her fingers.

With the door open, rain and leaves flying into the buggy, she glanced back for one last look at Matthew's handsome face.

He mirrored his sister's panicked look and shook his head. "*Nee*, Veronica. Stay here. You're safer with me."

She popped her head up to the windshield just enough to see that the man had his gun pointed at the buggy again. Another shot blasted through the windshield and she ducked. Relief engulfed her like a flash flood in a gully when it missed her and Esther, exiting out the back of the buggy and tearing a hole in the fiberglass.

"It's better for you this way." Tears threatened to mingle with the rain hitting her face. "Thank you," she whispered as she turned to the door. What she really wanted to say was "I love you," but it stuck in her throat. Now was not the time or place.

Before he could react, she reached across Esther, yanked the sliding door all the way open and pushed herself into the opening.

In that instant, time stood still. Was she really going to do it? Catapult herself out of a moving vehicle in the dark and the pouring rain?

Before her courage could disappear, Veronica dropped out of the buggy door. What seemed like an eternity as she was suspended in midair was actually a nanosecond, and she landed on the wet grass on the side of the road. Rolling several feet, she heard the buggy and the sedan continue on, the noise growing quieter. She stayed still on the grass for several seconds, the pain of hitting the ground reverberating throughout her body, and she evaluated herself for any injury. As the sound of the vehicles continue to fade, she stood up, feeling a little wobbly. With a long glance down the road and an urgent prayer for Matthew and Esther's safety as the reflective slow-moving-vehicle triangle faded into the darkness, she hurried into the woods. Pain stabbed her in the leg, and she slowed to a limp.

In the shelter of the trees, the rain wasn't as strong. But there was no way she was going back to the road despite the increasing darkness. Matthew and his sister would be safe now without her there. And there had to be something on the other side of these woods. Eventually, she'd come out and find a telephone. The US Marshal would keep her safe and get her another identity and another location, as well as catch Popov and return her to prison. Matthew Yoder would be a fond memory.

As she stumbled farther into the woods, determined that she would find her way in the morning, tears mingled with the raindrops on her cheeks.

It only took an instant for Matthew to decide he would follow her.

Time had stopped as he watched Veronica drop out the buggy door and roll into the grass to disappear into the woods. In the brief time he had known her, he had figured out she was a resilient and resourceful *maedel*. But in the woods, in the rain, in the dark of night? *Nee*, no one should attempt that alone.

He especially wouldn't abandon the woman he was falling in love with.

"Here." He thrust the reins into Esther's hands. "Head home. You'll be safe. They don't want you." Like most Amish *maedels*, she was a capable and skilled driver. And as soon as the occupants of the vehicle realized that Veronica was gone, the man would let go of the reins and his *schwester* could drive home to warmth and safety. With barely a glance at her startled expression, he grabbed the other blanket from the back seat and wiggled his way over Esther, who was now holding the reins and looking shell-shocked, but she scooted herself into the driver's seat.

Dickens had been well trained in pulling the buggy and had initially continued at his usual pace. But the horse had been startled by a car driving that closely, and his discomfort had eventually made him slow down. For that, Matthew thanked *Gott*.

With a quick second to fill his lungs with oxygen and a prayer for safety, he leaped from the moving buggy, landing on his good leg and forcing himself into a roll to break his fall.

He paused to take a few breaths and gather his strength before he stood, his hand covering the wound on his arm but a feeling of satisfaction washing over him at his ability to complete the feat. Glancing down the road, he saw that both the buggy and the car had slowed to a crawl. Apparently, the man had seen both he and Veronica jump out, for the car pulled away from the buggy.

Gut. Esther was safe.

Pushing himself up with his palms on the wet grass, rain soaking his hair and running down his face, he stood and turned to the woods. Upright, he paused for a few moments to get his balance, his disabled leg twitched with a spasm. He'd never done anything like that before, so he wasn't sure how his handicap would adjust to it. Truth be told, he'd only babied it since he'd recovered from the fire. And not just his leg, but he'd babied *himself*. Veronica had been the first person to need him to rediscover his physical abilities, to push him to more than he had thought himself capable. He shook his head to expel the rain from his hair and the romantic notions from his head. Later, after Veronica was safe, he could examine his heart and his feelings. Now, at least he hadn't landed his full weight on that leg. Only movement would tell him if he had been injured.

Gingerly, he took a step, pressing his weight on his leg,

a little at first until it held his entire weight. So far, so *gut*. He took another step and another without any pain.

His heart lighter with the assurance he had not been injured, he glanced down the road to see that the car had stopped. He needed to get moving.

A few of his short steps brought him to the edge of the woods. Keeping the blanket around his head, he looked back again to see the buggy continuing down the road but at a slower pace than before. Apparently, the man had let go of the horse's reins, and the car was now moving in reverse, the man's face peering into the dark, wet woods.

Esther would be safe. He exhaled a breath he hadn't realized he'd been holding.

Matthew trudged farther into the trees. His eyes adjusted to the darkness quickly, and he pushed branches out of his way, returning them to their natural positions gently so as not to draw attention to his location. Without his hat, though, rain pelted his face and dripped into his eyes. *"Veronica!"* He dared a hoarse whisper and prayed that the man didn't lower his window and hear him.

He continued to hobble deeper into the woods, whispering some more, searching for any type of movement that might indicate she was nearby.

No response.

Vehicle headlights swung past, illuminating the trees all around him. What were they doing? With the direction of the headlights, it seemed that the assailants had turned sideways on the road in order to shine the beams straight into the woods where he had disappeared.

His posture stiffened suddenly, his muscles going rigid as the headlights swung over and past him. Could the light have gone over him so quickly that they hadn't noticed a tall, gray column in the grass? He could only pray so.

He dropped to his knees, wincing with the sharp pain that hit the knee in his bad leg as well as the flesh wound on his arm and then forcing the discomfort out of his mind. Veronica needed him. He couldn't succumb to a little pain or he wouldn't be any good to her, now or in the future. Bending his face to the grass and making himself as small as he could, he pulled the gray blanket around him. "*Gott*, please make me look like a rock."

A car door creaked open. *Ach*, they were coming! With the sound of the pounding rain, Matthew was surprised he could hear it. He leaned forward, straining to hear what came next. Feet stepped through the grass, and branches at the side of the road flicked back and forth. Holding as still as possible, he continued to look ahead, searching for another gray blanket disguised as a rock. Maybe Veronica had had the same idea.

The footsteps continued to approach, although more slowly, until Matthew figured the man was only a few feet away. He must have only been looking for people running away and not the fuzzy rock right at his feet.

With a noisy exhalation of frustration, the man turned back and stomped through the underbrush back to his car.

Matthew waited a few more minutes. The lights swung away, and the sound of the motor faded into the distance. He couldn't hear the sound of a horse on the road, either, and he shot up another prayer for Esther's safety.

Slowly, he raised himself to standing and surveyed the area. Shaking water out of his hair and eyes, he realized his bookstore was only a couple of miles away. That meant going straight through the woods.

But did Veronica realize shelter was that close? Probably not.

With another glance down the road to reassure himself

that the sedan truly was gone and Esther was safely on her way back home, he pulled the blanket close and stepped farther into the woods.

Continuing on a narrow deer path several Amish used when they hunted, he noticed his leg wasn't dragging as much as it usually did. Had the additional physical activity actually helped him? Maybe his handicap wasn't as limiting as he had previously thought. An idea struck him out of nowhere. Could he be capable of leading a family? Of providing for them and caring for them and protecting them?

He pushed a tree branch to the side and scanned the area for Veronica. Ever since the accident, it had felt disloyal to his *mamm* and *daed* even to think about moving on from that tragedy. As if he could still save them if time did not move on. If his *life* did not move on.

And yet, what would his parents have wanted for him? They had encouraged his courtship, often expressing enthusiasm for future *boppli*. Maybe it would honor his parents to marry, to have lots of *boppli* and to raise up *kinner* in the Amish faith that *Mamm* and *Daed* had handed down to him.

Maybe he'd been going about this all wrong.

Urgency to find Veronica rose within him, propelling him through the darkness. If he got through the woods and to his bookstore without finding her, he would return at first light to continue looking, and pull in some other men to help in the search.

He stood to continue in the direction of his bookstore. A branch *thwapped* him across the cheek. He probed the spot and his fingers came away sticky. In the minuscule bit of light that fought for recognition in the middle of the rainstorm, it looked like blood. He had a first-aid kit at his bookstore. That would have to be good enough for this scrape and his bullet wound.

Worried thoughts accompanied him for several steps farther down the deer path, until his foot bumped something smack-dab in the middle of the walkway. A rock? How would that get there? He bent to feel its size. Could he move it out of the way, or should he go around it?

But the rock huddled at his feet was crying.

Veronica.

FOURTEEN

The smell of wet wool overpowered Veronica's senses, and she shivered as the blanket became more and more soaked, covering her back with the chill of dampness. She needed to get up and move on. Staying on the ground huddled under a wet blanket wouldn't get her safe and warm. It would only bring more trouble—but this time it would be her health at risk if she caught the flu or pneumonia or something worse from her time being exposed to the elements.

She mentally summoned all the strength she could muster, reminding herself of the promise she had made to her deceased parents and her living sisters hidden away somewhere with new identities under the witness protection program. No matter what it took, she would survive. She would fight with every ounce of strength and stamina she had, and she would continue on. Rather than wallowing in what was in the past, she would cling to the promise of a brighter future.

Her heartbeat stuttered. *Could she?*

Tears burst forth, and sobs of anguish wracked her body as she hugged herself tighter under the blanket. She let the grief roll over her, an emotion she rarely allowed herself.

Something jabbed her in the leg. She startled and scooted a couple of inches away from the intrusion. It moved on the ground and poked at her again. Her heart thrashing about, a scream rose in her throat—

"Veronica?"

She stilled, refusing to move a single muscle. Someone was there.

"Veronica, are you alright?"

Matthew? She recognized his voice, the gentleness of his tone and the bit of Amish accent. After pulling the blanket away from her face, she peeked out. In the darkness of the rainy night, she couldn't make out his features, but the man standing before her had the right height and the proper tilt to the side of his handicapped leg. "Matthew?"

"Jah." He reached out his hands.

She accepted his offer and leaned on his arms to stand. "You came for me?"

"For sure and for certain. I made a promise to myself back in the bus station that I would protect you."

Emotion overwhelmed her. He had come for her. She fell into his open arms and let the tears flow again, but this time against his chest. With some hesitation, his hands eventually found their way to stroke the back of her head. She slowly calmed, her sobs dissipating, her heart slowing to the pitter-patter of the rain, as she cherished the strength and safety of his embrace.

"Mein liebchen," he whispered under his breath, so quietly that Veronica wasn't sure she had heard him at all.

What did that mean? She wished she knew his Amish language.

In a louder voice, he asked, "Are you alright? Do you hurt anywhere?"

She jerked her head back with a gasp at the fresh realization that he was no longer in the buggy headed toward safety but had probably thrown himself out on the grass in order to follow her. Pulling away from him, she pounded a fist into his chest at the thought that he put himself in peril again. "What are you doing here?" Her voice sounded shrill and panicked to her ears and was probably loud enough to draw attention, but she couldn't seem to lower it. "I was trying to keep you safe by getting away from you and Esther. If I left, they would follow me, and you would be okay."

"*Ach*, I cannot leave a *maedel* in trouble." His soothing tone soaked into her, and she dropped her fist.

So that was it. She was just a female who needed help, and he was doing his duty as an Amish man of integrity to offer assistance when it was needed. Her chest constricted with the thought, but that was for the best. The two of them would never make a good pair, anyway, not with their vastly different backgrounds.

That settled that. She just needed a telephone and to reach her handler at the US Marshals Service, and she would be out of his way.

The rain began to lighten up, and she swiped a hand across her forehead, shifting the damp hairs back from her eyes. "Okay. Well, thank you, I think. Can you get us out of the woods and to a telephone?" A formality seeped into her attitude.

A look she couldn't quite see or identify flickered through his eyes at her crisp tone. "*Jah*, my bookstore is about a mile onward. I have a telephone there, remember? We were headed there in the buggy."

"Oh, yes." She felt limp as weariness tried to overtake her, and Matthew put an arm around her to hold her up. "My mind is such a muddled mess with everything that's happened that I'm losing track of where I am and where I'm going."

"*Jah*, that is understandable, to be *ferhoodled*." She heard his smile although she couldn't see it in the darkness.

"*Ferhoodled?* You're calling me that again?"

"*Jah*, you are confused. Or mixed up. Doesn't that sound about right?"

"Definitely." She peered through the darkness, relief flooding her that she had a guide now. "So, which way do we go?"

But then another thought struck her mind, and her heart leaped into her throat as she started trembling uncontrollably. "What if they find us?"

Matthew wanted to wrap his arms around her again but didn't dare after hearing the iciness that had crept into her tone. "They seemed unwilling to leave the sanctuary of their vehicle to chase through the unknown wet woods. I think we would have heard them following by now." He shook the rain out of his hair again. "In this case, the rain is helping us."

"Yeah. That makes sense." Slowly, she stopped trembling. "Do you know where we are?"

"*Jah*, I think so." A mental map of the area surfaced in his mind's eye with a pinpoint to the spot where he thought they were. "We're on the edge of the Hochstetler place. The mill we drove past earlier is just south of us. We could hole up there until the rain ends, but I think we ought to push on through to my bookstore. It's about the same distance."

Veronica shook water off the blanket and then settled it over her shoulders again. "How much more walking is it?"

"If I'm correct, it would be about thirty minutes under normal walking conditions. But we're in the dark and the rain, so it could take at least an hour." He gingerly reached out a hand to stroke her arm, praying it was a comfort and not an annoyance. Surely, she couldn't be irritated with him. He had done everything within his power to keep her safe. *Maedels* were such a mystery. Matthew forced himself to remain in the present moment and not get *ferhoodled* himself wondering whether he had misunderstood the signs that Veronica had some interest in him. She needed him here and now. "Can you make it alright?"

"Yes." She put a hand on his upper arm to steady herself and took a deep breath. But when she felt stable and pulled her hand away, she brought it close to her eyes to examine it. "Are you bleeding?"

In his gratitude for finding Veronica in one piece, he'd completely forgotten about being shot. Reaching his hand up to his bicep, he felt the edges of the ripped fabric of his shirt and the stickiness of fresh blood.

"*Jah*, the man in the car shot me. It is only a flesh wound. I don't think it hit the muscle." He held his sticky hand out in the rain to rinse the blood and then wiped his hand on his pants. All of his clothes would probably need to get thrown away eventually.

"You need medical care. What about a doctor?" She paused, an awkward moment hovering in the space between them, then plunged forward with the next question. "Do the Amish ever go to a hospital?"

He chuckled, a rippling from his core that refreshed him after the intensity of the evening. "*Jah*, we will go to a hospital when it is needed. Like most *Englisch*, we would rather not, but we do." A sudden heaviness claimed his limbs and his spirit as he remembered the truck and ambulance that had responded to the fire that killed his parents. They had been taken to the hospital, but the fire had done too much damage already. His *mamm* and *daed* had passed within minutes of their arrival at the institution that was supposed to heal them. "They don't always help."

Veronica put a hand on his forearm. "Are you alright?"

Her tone sounded as if she was asking about the wellness of his heart, but Matthew chose to take her question as if it was about his wound. "*Jah*, and I do not need a hospital. Nor a doctor. I have a first-aid kit at my bookstore. That will be sufficient for a superficial wound."

"Okay. So let's get there. Which way do we go?"

He grasped her shoulders and turned her around. "How about I lead?" He stepped around her and began in the proper direction.

A few moments into the hike, Veronica's voic sounded from some ways back. "Matthew? Are you up there?"

He halted and turned but could only see a shadowy figure several feet away. "*Jah*. Has something happened?"

"I can't see you well enough to follow." She stumbled forward and bumped into his back. Righting herself, she slid her hand down his arm until she could tuck her slender hand inside his larger one. "There. Now, I won't lose you."

Matthew's heart galloped at three times the speed of his feet as he held her hand and led her along the deer path. The rain eventually stopped, although they were completely soaked by the time he guided them from the trees. Lights flickered in the distance, a welcome sight as Matthew looked heavenward and thanked *Gott* that he had successfully navigated Veronica back to civilization. Now, if the *gut* Lord would keep them safe until Veronica could get in contact with the US Marshals Service, and if *Gott* could help him sort out his feelings for Veronica, he would never need to pray for anything else.

As they trudged into the light of the property of an auction house that held Amish mud sales, Veronica ran her free hand over her hair, grimacing. "I must look a mess." Her shoes squished as she slogged alongside him.

Matthew squeezed her fingers, momentarily forgetting the danger that had followed them for the last couple of days. "*Nee*, you are *schéin*."

"*Schéin?*" Her bungled pronunciation of the Pennsylvania German word was cute, but he hadn't meant to use another Amish word she would ask about. "What does that mean?"

He swallowed hard and nearly choked. Now, he was stuck, because he certainly wasn't going to lie. "It means you are beautiful."

Veronica's cheeks colored a light pink as she looked at the ground, running a hand across her hair again. She cleared her throat and then nodded toward the stores in the distance. "Is that where we're going?"

"*Jah*. All these businesses are run by Amish, but tourists like to shop here. My bookstore is at the far end." They were almost there. Almost to safety. Almost to the end of their time together.

But as he stepped out to cross a large empty field between the auction yard and the line of shops, a dark sedan pulled into the parking lot in the distance.

Matthew yanked Veronica back behind a tall pile of pallets. At her startled look, he whispered, "*Ach*, there's that car again."

She peered between the wood slats of the pallets, a shudder coursing over her. "I think you're right. Now what?"

Jah, exactly. Now what?

FIFTEEN

A frantic energy coursed through Veronica. She desperately wanted to bite her nails, but that was a bad habit she had fought to give up years ago. She refused to allow the current stress to start it again.

Matthew stood watching the vehicle for what seemed like an eternity, as it turned in a circle in the parking lot, its headlights sweeping over the stack of crates that hid them. But it didn't leave. It stayed put, its lamps illuminating a set of tractors just a couple of yards from their hiding spot.

"Shouldn't we find a better hiding place?" she hissed. It sounded harsher than she intended, but fear enveloped her like her wet blanket.

"*Jah, gut* idea. Let's find shelter." He turned in a complete circle, surveying the equipment nearby.

From what Veronica could see, there wasn't much available. Some farming equipment that looked like it would be pulled by horses stood nearby, but every piece had an open seat. That wouldn't hide them. There was also an open-bed trailer that looked like a stage platform, but the only way that could camouflage them was if they crawled underneath. No way did she want to lie down in the mud again if there was another option.

"There." He nodded toward a lone buggy several feet

away. "That enclosed buggy can hide us and keep us out of the rain."

He watched the sedan a few seconds longer. When it didn't move, he whispered, "Now."

Veronica grabbed his hand again, taking comfort and warmth from his strength, and followed him at a quick pace until they were in the buggy, then Matthew pulled the door closed behind them. The back of the buggy faced the parking lot, so only a small window in the back could reveal their position. Veronica moved to peek out the window at the same time as Matthew, and their heads clunked.

"Sorry," she whispered as she moved away, rubbing her head.

"The car is still there." He ducked down from the window. "And we are back in a buggy again, but at least we're out of the rain."

"I like buggies. They're cozy." She spread her skirt out as much as she could on the bench so it could dry, then pulled the blanket tighter about her shoulders. It would be even better if she could have dry clothes. The image of riding in the buggy with Matthew, clean and dry and her hair fixed in the Amish way, with someplace to go that didn't involve danger, rose unbidden in her mind. She shook her head in the vain hope of expelling the notion and looked out the front storm shield toward the farm equipment. "What is this place?"

"This is where our community holds mud sales."

Veronica chuckled. "Well, there's plenty of mud to sell."

"Nee." Matthew smiled. "We don't sell mud. All these things here, including this buggy, will be auctioned off in another couple of weeks. Some families and businesses set up booths to sell food and quilts and furniture. It all benefits our volunteer fire department."

"Sounds fun."

"It is. I think you'd like it. They're usually held in the spring, when it's muddy, hence the name. This one's a little unusual in the summer." He peeked out the back window again, and Veronica moved to see as well, their cheeks nearly touching. The car was still there, but it had moved slightly, its lights shining closer to the buggy where they hid.

"What do we do if they see us?" She turned to look at Matthew, her face just a couple of inches from his. Being this close to him, she felt she could barely breathe. His woodsy scent tickled her nose.

"We run." He shifted toward her, his lips dangerously close to hers. "We pray."

Time seemed to stop as something indefinable, something *mysterious*, hung between them. Was he going to kiss her? Veronica wanted to close her eyes in anticipation, but she couldn't look away from Matthew's rich brown eyes. She hadn't known him long, but it seemed as if he could see all the way through her to her soul.

He moved toward her, millimeter by millimeter.

Suddenly, the light pierced the window and swept over their faces. Veronica jerked away, shrinking herself into the corner of the back seat. Matthew ducked down, too, as the light moved across the back of the buggy.

After a few moments of darkness, he raised his head enough to see the parking lot. "The car is gone."

Her heart beat a staccato rhythm inside her chest. "Are we safe?"

"I believe so. For now." He ran a hand through his hair, ruffling it. "Maybe now we can get to my shop. You should be safe there."

Physically, maybe. But the moment between them had passed, most likely never to return. Once she contacted her handler and he came for her, she would never see Matthew again.

That meant her heart wouldn't be safe.

It would be broken.

Ach, he'd really missed a *wunderbaar* opportunity.

When he had been a teenager, Matthew had made the mistake of not staying close enough to the hindquarters of a horse as he walked behind it. The result had been a kick to his chest. By the horse's standards, it had been a light tap, a warning not to get too near. But it had knocked Matthew off his feet and left a large bruise that took several weeks to heal. His *daed* had rushed him to the hospital, but thank *Gott*, it hadn't been serious.

This missed opportunity with Veronica, when he could have said something, *anything*, about how he felt about her, when he could have kissed her, felt like a deeper injury than that kick to the chest. As he led her across the auction yard and toward his bookstore, he rubbed that same spot with his hand as if that would soothe the deep pain.

But this blow wouldn't heal like the kick from the horse. This one hit harder and closer to the heart. It was a knockout from which he wasn't sure he could recover.

He stopped at the edge of the shops to check behind them for the dark sedan. With no vehicle in sight, he led Veronica along the backside, out of sight of the main road in case anyone drove past. All the stores had closed well over an hour ago and now sat dark and empty. The street also was fairly quiet. Everything shut down early in Amish communities.

At the back door of his store, he pulled an artificial red geranium out of its pot. From the underside of the plastic dirt, he retrieved a small metal case. In the melee at

his house, he hadn't thought to grab the key to the building, so he slid open the key holder, dumped the key into
his hand and opened the door, allowing Veronica to step
inside first. He returned the key holder to the pot, but he
pocketed the key.

Inhaling deeply of the soothing scent of paper and books,
Matthew followed Veronica inside. "Let's leave the lights
off so no one knows we're here. It's dark, but I can lead us
to the office and the telephone."

"Lights? You have electricity in here?"

"*Jah*, for the *Englisch* customers. They want to see how
we Amish live, but they usually don't want to experience
it for themselves. So our bishop allows it for businesses."

The small space just inside the back door acted as a back
porch, a place to leave packages or dirty shoes or hats, or
in their case, *wet blankets*. Matthew pulled a couple of tow-
els out of a nearby cabinet, and Veronica eagerly applied
one to her hair.

"Okay, first things first." Her voice was muffled by the
towel over her head. "Where's that first-aid kit you mentioned?"

Finally feeling a bit more comfortable as he continued
to dry out, he retrieved the medical supplies from a cabinet
and then grasped her soft hand again for the short distance
to the office behind the counter. A tiny bit of light filtered
through the uncovered windows, but Matthew had spent
so much time running his bookshop he could have found
his way around blindfolded.

He opened the door to a tiny office space and settled
Veronica in the only chair, the one behind his desk that
was covered with neat stacks of paper. She sat and sighed
deeply, the sound of a mixture of relief and exhaustion.
After a look around the small windowless room, which

contained only his desk and chair, a metal filing cabinet and a clock and a calendar on the plain white walls, she asked, "How is it you have a phone here?"

Matthew grabbed a stool from behind the counter and pulled it into the office. "Telephones are permitted for business purposes. We need them to communicate with *Englisch* suppliers and customers. It is at home that telephones are not allowed."

"What's wrong with a phone at home? It sure would be convenient." Veronica put her fingers on the corners of the stack of papers closest to her to straighten it.

"*Jah*, probably so. Every once in a while someone brings it up with the bishop." He perched on the stool and opened the first-aid kit. "But a telephone would also provide too much connection to the outside world and could pull our families and home life apart."

"I admire that determination." She gently cleaned his wound with an antiseptic wipe. "I spend a ton of time on my phone. Or at least I used to, before I forgot it in my apartment. Social media, videos, just looking up information. I really miss it." She pulled a tube of ointment out of the kit, a thoughtful look on her face. "Or at least I did at first. I'm rather getting used to it now, being unplugged."

"*Jah?* So you understand why our community doesn't allow phones?"

She nodded. "I've actually read a lot of articles and posts on social media about how cell phones pull people apart and estrange teens from their parents. So, yeah, I can see a lot of sense in the Amish decision."

"There's a district near here where the youth increasingly have cell phones. It's not going well for them."

"That's sad. Family is one of our biggest blessings." A tear escaped, and Veronica swiped at her face.

Was she thinking of the sisters she had mentioned earlier? Losing one's parents was difficult. He knew that well enough from his own experience. But to be separated from siblings also? He couldn't imagine that additional distress.

She finished applying the bandage and closed the kit. After scooting the stool closer to the desk, he grabbed the telephone. In a brief call with the police department, he described the attack at his house and their subsequent escape. A couple of units were dispatched to his home, and they called back to report that they hadn't found anyone there and the house was secure. If no one was there, where was Esther?

Matthew pressed his lips tight as his stomach clenched. There was nothing more they could do. That meant Popov and her henchman were still on the loose and Veronica remained in danger.

"Sir?" The officer's voice in his ear broke through his thinking. "Are you alright where you are? We can send a police cruiser around to check on you."

In the quiet of the office, the man's voice came through the receiver loudly, and Veronica's eyes stretched wide at his suggestion. She shook her head vigorously.

"Nee." He cleared his throat. "No, but thank you. We are fine." A police vehicle outside his bookstore could alert Popov to their location. "I will call again if we need you."

Veronica rubbed her hands over her drooping eyes. "Now what?"

"We can't go back to my house."

"Definitely not. Not now that Popov knows where you live." She blew out a breath. "I'm so sorry to have brought all this on you. I never should have jumped into the minivan back at the bus station."

"Nee, I am glad you did. Danger aside, you have added

some excitement to my life. This is the type of adventure I've only read about. And I hope I have been able to help."

Veronica pressed a hand to her cheek as if she was blushing. "'For sure and for certain,' as you say. I am still alive and free." Her smile shone through the dimness.

"So I think taking you to stay at a friend's house would not only be super awkward for you since you don't know any of my friends but also impossible since I have no transportation." Matthew shifted on the stool. "However, there's a small apartment above the bookstore, just big enough for a sitting area, a tiny kitchen, a bedroom and bathroom."

Veronica clasped her hands together. "Terrific! We can stay there. Shower. Sleep. Maybe eat if you have any food, but I think I saw a sales rack of candy on our way through the store so we at least have that." She smiled. "And then we can call the US Marshals Service in the morning."

He rubbed the back of his neck. "*Jah.* I'll take the sofa in the sitting area." His mind could not conceive of what the bishop might say of the two of them staying the night in his apartment, but what other choice did he have? The circumstances were most unusual, and he did not want to leave her alone. Besides, where would he go, and how would he get there?

The telephone rang, making him jump from the stool with the loud noise in the small space. He dried his sweaty palms on his shirt and then grabbed the receiver. "*Jah?*"

"Matthew? *Mein bruder?* You are safe?" Esther's voice calmed him like a soothing balm of ointment.

"*Jah*, we are well. Where are you? What happened after we jumped out of the buggy?" He whispered to Veronica that it was Esther, and she smiled broadly as she sagged in the chair with relief. Matthew held out the receiver so Veronica could hear as well.

"I am *gut*. It was just as you said it would be. When Veronica and then you left the buggy, the man in the car released Dickens and let me alone. I continued on, and when I was sure they weren't following me, I drove to my friend Sarah's house. She was quite startled, of course, to hear everything, but I'm staying with her. I figured it would be okay to use the telephone in their barn to call you. I know how you worry, *bruder*."

Heat rose up his neck as Veronica smiled at him, her head tilted as if filing that bit of information away for future use.

"It is *gut* to hear your voice, *mein schwester*. I will be in contact with you tomorrow." As he replaced the receiver in its cradle, he rubbed a hand over his face, suddenly unsure if he'd be able to eat anything despite his growing hunger.

He would not have labeled himself a worrier, but he had to admit, if only to himself, that the current situation made him fret. Of course, he knew the Scripture about how tomorrow has enough worries of its own, but he couldn't stop the ping-pong of thoughts intruding in his head.

What would happen tomorrow? And what if he failed in protecting Veronica?

SIXTEEN

Veronica soon felt settled into Matthew's cute and cozy upstairs apartment, sipping on chicken noodle soup by the low light and warmed by a bit of heat from a propane lamp. She had been quite surprised that the Amish bachelor had canned goods in a place where he didn't live, and she had been quick to check the expiration date on the container of soup, especially since she recognized that the manufacturer had changed the design of the label a while ago.

Now, drowsiness engulfed her, although she didn't want to go to bed without cleaning up the kitchen. As he finished his soup, Matthew stood and asked, "Do you want some *kaffee*?"

As tired as she was, she was not eager for this time with him to end. "Coffee? Sure, that sounds good."

As the coffee perked, he placed two mugs and an old plastic container of sugar on the table between them. "When I was in a restaurant with my *schwester* and my *aendi* and *oncle* a while back, I heard an *Englisch* man ask a woman, 'so what brings a nice girl like you to a place like this?' It sounded incredibly awkward at the time, but it's a valid question sometimes." He cleared his throat. "I would be most curious to hear about the real Veronica and how she came to be running for her life. You already told me that you witnessed a kidnapping ring in a department store and saw your parents murdered. But is there more?"

His intense brown eyes pierced her. Could she trust him with the whole story? She wasn't supposed to tell anyone, at all, *ever*, or her life could be in danger.

But nothing would ever be the same again. Her life already was in jeopardy, and she didn't seem to have any power over her current circumstances, let alone her future. Why not unburden her soul?

He poured the coffee, and as she spooned in the sugar, she avoided his gaze. Somehow, it seemed that it would be easier, safer, after twenty years of hiding, to tell the truth without making eye contact. And she was in desperate need of feeling safe. Her mind wandered for a moment. What would it be like to feel completely safe and protected? She wasn't really sure. But if the sense of comfort she had when she was around Matthew was any indication, she would live with the Amish for the rest of her days.

"There's more." She sighed. "While my parents shopped, my two sisters and I played inside the clothing racks. We were pretty good at getting in without messing up all the clothing, and it was a tremendous hiding spot." She smiled at the memory of the tingling sensation on her skin as she pushed through the dresses, shirts and pants on the hangers, and the warmth of being inside that cocoon of clothing. Even now, she could still see clearly her sisters grinning as they planned their game. "As we came out to move to another clothing rack, I witnessed a woman snatch a little child out of a shopping cart while the mother's back was turned."

"That woman was Nadia Popov, the one who is chasing you now?"

"Yes." Veronica wrapped her hands around her mug,

seeking its comforting warmth. "She handed that child off to a man in another aisle, and he disappeared with the little girl. I was only ten, but I knew that what I had seen wasn't right. Our parents had ingrained in us that we should speak up when a wrong was done to someone. Protect those who can't defend themselves."

"*Jah*, that is wise advice." Matthew's eyes twinkled at her from across the table. "The Amish teach that to their children as well, and we put it into practice when we can."

"Like me?" Her shoulders slumped, and she traced her fingertip around the edge of the mug. "I never thought I'd be the one who needed protecting."

"Everyone needs help from time to time. I was in the right place at the right time to be of assistance." His warm smile spread a lightness through her chest as he waved away the significance of what he had done for her. "I distracted you from your story."

"We were going to tell our parents, since we figured they would know what to do. But as we peeked out of the hiding spot in the clothing rack, we saw—mostly me, since I was the one in front—the kidnappers gun down our parents." Veronica swallowed hard but couldn't keep back the tears. The memories had remained as vivid as if it was happening right then, all over again.

Matthew released his mug and put both of his warm hands over hers. "*Ach*, I am so sorry you had to witness that."

"We hid in the clothing rack until the police arrived and managed to get us to come out. They immediately took us into custody, and then my sisters and I testified against Popov at her trial." She swiped the tears off her cheeks. "After that, the US Marshals Service placed us in the witness protection program, but separated us. Since they never found her accomplice, they thought it would be safer if we were not together."

"I suppose."

"I guess they thought Popov's partner in crime would be looking for three sisters, or that we might talk if we were together. It can be difficult for little girls to keep secrets." Despite her grief, a smile broke through her tears.

"You had no choice but to trust the US Marshals then. Are you having difficulty trusting them now?" Matthew released her hands to sip from his mug. "And no judgment here, as you *Englischers* like to say. The Amish have a general distrust of *Englisch* law enforcement as well. We prefer to handle our difficulties on our own."

Could she be completely honest with him? She clutched her hands to her chest as the chill created by Matthew's withdrawal seeped in. But what did she have to lose? He had been with her every step of the way, comforting and encouraging her. They would go their separate ways soon enough. She wanted to soak up as much warmth and support as she could so the memories might sustain her in the lonely days to come.

"Trust is not one of my strengths right now." A self-deprecating laugh bubbled out, sounding awkward between them. "To tell the whole truth and nothing but the truth, so help me God, I've been living a fake life. That's what witness protection does. They strip away the old you, create a new you, and off you go into another life, frantically trying to remember who you are from day to day until the lies seep down deep and you can barely remember the truth of who you used to be. And if my life is made up, how can I trust anyone else to be genuine? How can I trust God to be who He says He is?"

"*Jah*, that is a valid question for believers and nonbelievers both." Matthew refilled his coffee mug and gestured to her to see if she wanted some, but she shook her head.

"I remember going to Sunday school with my sisters and my parents talking about their faith, encouraging us girls to believe." She ran a hand over her hair as if that would calm her pounding heart. "I used to believe. But the horror of my parents' murders, being pulled away from my sisters, living as I do—all that has made me doubt. I've never been ready to give up on God completely." She thought for a moment, and Matthew was kind to let her think. An idea pinged in her brain. "God is like the book at the bottom of my to-be-read pile. I'll get to it eventually, but there are too many other things to do or read first."

"Sometimes, though, we need to reevaluate our lists and reshuffle them. Maybe there's a book that's shifted to the bottom, but when we take another look at it, months or maybe years after we first put it on the stack, we realize we're ready for it now." He set his mug on the table. "It's okay to pull books from the bottom of the stack." He smiled, and the teasing twinkle in his eyes shone forth again.

"I see your point." Maybe the brain fog was beginning to lift. "But I think I need to figure out who I am before I try to figure out who He is. And after the past couple of decades, I'm not sure anymore." She huffed out a breath. "When a government agency can issue a new birth certificate and a new driver's license and a new Social Security card at their whim, it messes with your sense of identity."

"*Nee.* As you learn more about who *Gott* is, you will discover who He made you to be."

"You think so?"

"*Jah*, for sure and for certain. Those are just pieces of papers with numbers. They don't determine who you are.

Gott decided that when He knit you in your mother's womb, and then your life is your own, not someone else's. We have a saying that every man must live with the man he makes of himself." He leaned forward and reached out like he wanted to touch her, but he stopped short, an expression of longing mingled with discomfort stretched across his face. "You and *Gott* have power over who you are, not the State of Indiana when they issue a birth certificate and then a driver's license."

Her coffee had gone cold, but she took a sip anyway. What Matthew said made sense. Everything he said was steeped in wisdom. What was she going to do when she went back to her WITSEC life without him?

"You're right, of course." She stifled a sigh and summoned the wherewithal to gaze into his intense brown eyes. "My time with you in the Amish community has been healing and peaceful. I think, perhaps, I should give God another chance in my life."

But *could* she? He smiled at her response, and she couldn't stop from admitting, only to herself, how much she had begun to care for Matthew. Would it be possible for them to have a future together?

He stood and touched her shoulder as he moved past her to a closet. Then, after pulling out a blanket and pillow, he began to make up the sofa.

His kindness and his accommodation of her needs overwhelmed her. Were all Amish like that?

But then a knot formed in her midsection and she inhaled sharply, unable to fill her lungs completely. When she had been emancipated from the foster care system at the age of eighteen, she had decided that no matter how much she wanted a relationship and a family, it was better to be alone. Her jaw was set and her shoulders thrown back as she couldn't renege on that promise she had made to herself.

She watched Matthew unfold and shake out the blanket, reluctantly noticing his broad shoulders and his strength in something as simple as making a bed. But even now, with this handsome and kind man right here seemingly interested in more than just helping her survive, she couldn't commit to a relationship.

The danger she had feared all those years had finally arrived, and it was worse than she had imagined. She had met a man who intrigued her, but he lived such a life of truth that she could never be good enough for him. Not when she had been living lies for so long. She may be able to figure out her identity as God saw her, but her past made a romance with Matthew completely unthinkable.

With his back to her, Veronica closed her eyes and lowered her head as memories of what she saw that night her parents were murdered invaded her mind. Her stomach roiled, and she shivered with the sensation of an ice cube sliding down her spine. Lots of therapy, courtesy of the US Marshal Service, still could not keep away the bad dreams.

Then strong arms encircled her, lifting her to her feet. Matthew turned her to face him, his protective arms feeling powerful enough to keep out all the bad thoughts and memories. As soon as the tears began, she knew she would not be able to contain them. She sobbed into his shoulder, savoring the peace that now surrounded her.

Maybe with the memory of this moment she could find the strength to move into the next chapter of her life.

Matthew tossed and turned through the wee hours of the morning on the sofa in the tiny apartment. His restlessness was due mostly to his vigilance in listening and watching for any suspicious activity in the bookstore below, or around the building's outside perimeter. But he had to admit some of it was due to his conversation with the beautiful *maedel*. He had surprised himself with how easily his reassurances about her faith had rolled out of his brain and off his tongue, especially since he'd had so many serious doubts of his own.

In those night hours, he'd whispered many prayers for his and Veronica's safety, but also for Esther. He had struggled plenty with how a *Gott* who loved and cared for His people could allow his parents to die in that horrible *haus* fire. But his little *schwester* had reminded him that *Gott* had some purpose in everything and was working it together for his *gut*.

"If you don't believe all of the Bible, then don't believe any of it," she had said to him. "Are you ready to renounce your faith, including your Amish life, because of that tragedy?"

He had not hesitated to say *nee*, he would not leave the Amish church. His faith had grown in leaps and bounds since that conversation, and he did not want to leave the Amish, no matter how beautiful and thoughtful and kind the *Englisch* woman was.

At daybreak, he rose and immediately went around to each window to check for any threats. All had been quiet through the night, except for a mild wind that made a tree branch scratch at the window. But he was familiar with that sound, and it didn't seem to have bothered Veronica. All looked secure now, but he stood at the window facing the back, listening for anything out of the ordinary and watching the tree line. After several minutes of normality, he headed to the kitchenette.

It only took a few minutes to fold his blanket and dry the

dishes he had washed and left on the drying pad the night before. It was not the way his *mamm* had taught him. She had always insisted that everything be dried and put away before the kitchen was considered *redd up*. But he figured that, as a bachelor, he could be allowed a few changes.

Englischers slept later than the Amish did, and with Veronica still sleeping, Matthew crept downstairs. He double-checked the lock on both the front and the back doors, and all looked secure through the first-floor windows as well. With the one entrance to the upstairs apartment within sight from his office, he used the telephone to call Esther's friend. He wasn't up-to-date on all the bishop's rules about personal telephone use since he hadn't any need for personal calls. Not like so many of the womenfolk who liked to chatter about the community happenings. He wouldn't call it gossip, per se, but it did seem to come close. Surely, under these circumstances, the bishop would approve his use of the telephone.

Since her friend's family was up early as well, taking care of their animals and getting their day's work started, there was someone to hear the phone ring and fetch Esther. A few minutes of conversation assured him that she was well and there had not been any trouble in the night. He reassured her that he did not expect any danger for her or her hosts since she had nothing to do with Veronica's situation. With a promise from his little *schwester* that she would be praying for their safety, he hung up.

The floor above him squeaked, and then a door closed. Veronica must be up.

Matthew took some time to straighten a few piles of papers on his desk and return the telephone to its spot against the wall to give her some time to prepare for the day without his interfering and possibly uncomfortable presence.

After a few more squeaks of the floor above as he looked through a pile of invoices, he checked the clock, the only decorative item on the wall besides the calendar for the current year. Veronica had had fifteen minutes by herself. He'd lived with a mother and then a sister all his life, so he knew that probably wasn't enough time for a female. But when his stomach rumbled so loudly he was afraid it could be heard outside, he left the Closed sign on the door and returned upstairs to the apartment to fix breakfast.

Veronica stood at the stove, a spatula in hand, eggs, sausage, cheese and spices all frying together in a skillet. A wary look flashed across her face as he opened the door at the top of the stairs, but then a smile broke through as recognition dawned.

"Gut morge." His voice came out sounding more gravelly than normal.

"Good morning? I think I remember that's what Esther said when she gave me these clothes." She glanced down at her dress.

"Wunderbaar! Jah, good morning." It would not take long at all for him to get used to a pretty wife cooking breakfast for him, especially one who was such a talented chef. A pang struck him in the chest. If only that was a possibility.

Breakfast was a limited affair due to the lack of complete supplies in the apartment. He longed for milk or a fruit juice. Eggs didn't taste quite as good with water to wash them down. He barely noticed the flavor, though, with the distraction of Veronica sitting across from him.

Too soon, they had completed the meal and then watched the clock for the opening of the business day, so Veronica could call the US Marshals office. The ticktock of the wall clock and the splash of the water in the sink were the only sounds as they washed the breakfast dishes. The sense of time passing pressed on him, urging him to say something—*anything*—so Veronica would know how he felt about her. Maybe he could keep this relationship going, even after WITSEC took her back.

Was that even an option, though? Perhaps WITSEC would give her a new name, a new background, a new identity and move her to a different city. If she disappeared into the system, that would finish off whatever this relationship was budding into. He would never see her again.

Veronica swiped the sponge over a plate one more time and handed it to Matthew. As he took it in his grasp, his fingers touched hers. A current of electricity ran from her to him, and she jolted away, breaking the connection.

Jah, that was confirmation enough that she also knew nothing could come of their growing affection.

He quickly wiped the plate and placed it back in the cabinet as Veronica washed the last *kaffee* mug. As he put away the cup and pushed the cabinet door closed with a click, another sound came from the window. He paused and stood still to listen. Was it just the sound of the latching mechanism?

Veronica turned to him, panic etched into the lines around her eyes, her knuckles white as she clutched the dishrag. "Did you hear something?" Her hoarse whisper occupied the space between them.

He nodded, refusing to make any sound, lest they be heard. He should have figured—*jah*, he had but he hadn't wanted to admit it—their hiding space would not remain safe for long. If only he had transportation. But Esther had taken the buggy last night, and he didn't dare tiptoe down the stairs to use the telephone to call for the Amish taxi.

A rattling, the noise of tin cans clanking against each

other like he had heard at his house right before they had been attacked, sounded throughout the building. He immediately swung his gaze to Veronica. She nodded, a look of chagrin lighting her face.

Her early warning system had worked again.

He didn't want to ask her and risk being heard, but it sounded like Popov and her cohort were at the back door to the store. If he and Veronica descended the stairs from the apartment, they would come down directly across from that back entryway. They would walk directly into danger. *Jah*, peril had plagued them for a couple of days now, but they had not sought it out. Going down those steps would be a surefire way to get shot.

If they could get to the ground outside while their attackers were in the store, they might have a chance of escape. But how?

The front window wouldn't work. It had been stuck shut and on Matthew's to-do list for months. Now was not the time to fight that problem.

He crossed to the back window, praying to *Gott* that his lame leg wouldn't prevent him from keeping Veronica safe. A single purple clematis bloom rose its head to the windowsill. *Ach*, the trellis. He wished he'd thought of it earlier. Last year, Esther, who always wanted to plant more flowers, had insisted that he stake a trellis at the window. It had been a sturdy wooden thing, taller than most, and he had not been enthusiastic about setting it up. The abilities of his *schwester*'s green thumb did not equal her love for plants. But like a *gut* big *bruder*, he had complied.

Now, he would be sure to give her a *kusse* on the cheek for providing their escape.

He gestured to Veronica, surveying the area through the window to verify that no one would see them and catch them at the bottom. She smiled when she saw the trellis and raised the window. A fresh morning breeze lifted her hair, infusing hope into Matthew's spirit. Clutching her Amish skirts in one hand, she put a leg through the window and onto the top rung of the wooden trellis. It stood strong, thanks to Matthew's work in securing it to the building when he put it up.

She swung her other leg out and moved down a rung, her hands grasping the windowsill. "I think it'll work," she whispered.

He shook his head at his own lack of leadership, *ferhoodled* at how she had managed to get out the window first. After crossing back to the apartment door, he listened intently. The footsteps sounded like their attackers were completely inside and moving about the bookstore now.

Back at the window, he peered out to see Veronica one third of the way down the trellis. So far, it held steady. It was his turn now.

With a couple of oxygen-rich breaths to bolster his determination, he sat on the windowsill and grasped his injured leg with both hands to lug it across the threshold of the window. Maneuvering his foot to the top rung of the trellis, he shifted his weight to balance on the outside of the window. Grasping the edge of the opening, he brought the other limb through and stood on the top support.

Leading with his good leg, he lowered himself another two rungs, the meager leaves of the clematis tickling his hands and wrists. Veronica looked to be halfway down already.

As he placed his foot on the next rung down, a loud splintering sounded as his shoe crashed through the wood support. He grasped the rung above him, desperate to hold himself steady as his lame leg began to tremble with the effort of holding his entire body weight.

The memory of the fire that killed his parents rose unbidden. He had climbed to the upper story in an effort to save his parents, but his strength had faltered as smoke overwhelmed him. The fall to the ground had cost his parents their lives. He hadn't been able to save them, no matter how hard he'd tried.

Heat rose in him at the remembrance. He set his jaw. He would *not* fail Veronica.

But then, the wooden rung holding his entire weight shattered under his leg. Sweat broke out on his brow as he grabbed for a better grip with his hands. Perspiration slicked his palms, his grip slipping.

How long could he hold on? He felt around with his toe for another rung for his feet, but there was nothing.

In a moment, he would plummet to the ground, failing both himself and Veronica.

SEVENTEEN

This was it. This was where it would all end. All of that running and protecting would be for nothing. They would either kill themselves in a fall, or Popov and her thug would capture them at the bottom and haul them away.

Matthew's finger slipped a fraction of an inch, and he flailed his foot, looking for a place to land. Had Veronica broken the trellis on her way down? He couldn't ask. The risk of being heard was too great.

Peering over his arm, he twisted to see behind him and down below. So far, it seemed they had not been discovered. A hawk screeched as it dove down for a kill, piercing the quiet that lay over the fields in the midmorning hours. Wistfulness twisted in his chest. If only he could be a bird and fly away.

A bee buzzed up to his face. Instinctually, he jerked away. That head movement threw off his balance, and his fingers slipped a few millimeters more.

Slowly, he turned to look at his fingers again. Matthew had no idea he had so much strength in them, but his best guess was that he only had a few seconds more. He moved his feet around but could not find a grip for his toes.

"Matthew?" Veronica's whisper sounded strangely calm. "If you let go, there's another rung a few inches below your feet. Land on that and grab the next rung down with your hands. You'll be fine."

He wanted to look down to see where she was, but wasn't willing to risk slipping even farther. A crash from inside the upstairs apartment reached his ears. If he could see over the windowsill, he could make a threat assessment, but he had fallen too far. If Popov's partner had kicked in the door, he and Veronica had only a few seconds before bullets would rain down from the upstairs window.

And then it happened.

In a heartbeat, his window of opportunity to make a decision disappeared. Perspiration slicked his palms and fingers, and his grip slipped completely.

His mind flailed as he went into a free fall.

"Grab the trellis!" Veronica didn't bother to whisper this time.

Her voice kicked his brain into gear. Opening his palms, he grasped for the feel of a strong wooden rung in his hand, pointing his toes inside his shoes to catch the stopping place on his way down.

Time paused as the falling sensation stretched over him.

And then, he had it. A wooden rod touched his palm. He grabbed it, jerking his other hand up to the same level.

His toes hit a solid surface beneath him at an impact that nearly folded them backward inside his shoes. Whatever. He would deal with the pain and possible injury later. He had stopped falling. He wouldn't plummet to his death on the hard dirt below, taking Veronica with him. Survival was the most important thing right now, and it seemed he would live to see at least a few more minutes.

He inhaled and held the breath, counting one-two-three to settle his heart rate back down to a healthy level. "*Denki, Gott,*" he whispered to himself.

Loud steps pounded in the room above them. Matthew tried to shake the trellis rung to check its sturdiness and, satisfied with how solid the wood was both in his hands and under his feet, twisted again to look down over his arm at Veronica. Her face was pale with distress, her irises tiny black specks in the wide green of her eyes.

He had managed to stop himself within just inches of Veronica's head. *Ach*, no wonder she looked so panicked.

The steps pounded again, this time stopping directly overhead.

"*Goh*, Veronica! Go! Quickly!"

The look of terror didn't disappear, but she began moving down the trellis, picking up speed. A couple of rungs and a few feet from the ground, she jumped, landing solidly on both feet. "Come on," she urged him. "They're in the window!"

Matthew wouldn't take the time to look up. His leg aching, he lowered his strong leg onto the rung below, moving his hands down as well. Did they have a gun pointed at him? Sweat dampened his shirt, and he swallowed hard in a vain effort to keep the fear away.

His disabled limb came next. He rested it on the rung as briefly as he could while he swung down his hands and threw his body weight onto the strong leg again. Veronica stood at the bottom, urging him on. His heart crumpled within him, the possibility of failing Veronica rearing its ugly head again like an unruly and untrained horse.

He couldn't stop now. She needed him. Pushing the limits of his endurance, he strained his legs and forearms to get down the rest of the way. One thing mattered—Veronica's survival.

A crack sounded above him. Suddenly, a bullet whizzed past his head and struck the ground next to Veronica.

Move faster, he urged himself.

Ignoring the risk to his leg, he let loose of the trellis and dropped the last few feet onto the hard ground. Sharp pain ricocheted up from his heel past his knee. His leg gave way under the agony, and he dropped into a roll. He stood up on his solid leg, then held out his arms for balance for the few nanoseconds he could allow.

"Are you okay?" Veronica scanned him from head to toe, her head cocked to the side as she examined him.

"*Jah*, I better be." He grabbed her hand. "We need to get out of here."

He turned them away from the house and toward the cornfield. Within a few loping steps, another shot sped from the upstairs window. It hit the ground inches away from Veronica's foot.

"Can you go any faster?" She matched his pace, a look of compassion on her face.

"*Jah.*" Sweat trickled down the side of his cheek. He put his weight on his injured leg, trying to tell himself that he could do it, but misgivings bit at him like a swarm of mosquitoes.

With a final push for the last several feet, he broke through the mature cornstalks, maintaining a desperate grasp of Veronica's hand. By midsummer, a good corn crop could easily be as tall as an average man. Far enough in, the stalks would be thick enough to hide them from sight.

As Matthew shoved some aside in order to fit through, he noted with satisfaction that the stalks were just taller than him and could hide them both. *Denki, Gott!*

"Will this hide us?" Veronica whispered.

"*Jah*, should, when we stop trampling it."

He paused for a moment to listen. Their pursuers crashed through the stalks behind them, although it sounded as if they were quite some distance away. Surely, they wouldn't fire blindly into the corn. He couldn't imagine the mind or the decisions of an evil person like those two must be. He could only pray.

As they listened, the crunching of the stalks behind them slowed.

He held out his hand, palm out, to stop her from continuing on. Their escape through the field would damage the maturing corn, and for that, he had great regret. But he couldn't help it now. Staying alive was of utmost importance.

"Are they gone?" Veronica asked, her quiet voice like the whisper of the wind.

Matthew leaned to the right and to the left, trying to see through the tall stalks. He shrugged and then nodded, trying to communicate that he thought so, but wasn't sure. All remained quiet as they waited.

To be perfectly honest with himself, he was grateful for the rest. His tumble down the trellis had made his leg throb, and he wasn't sure how quickly he could walk or how far he could *goh*. They needed to move on. Even though Matthew couldn't hear movement, it was possible that Popov and her thug could smash through the corn at any moment. If that happened, he had no idea what he would do.

Veronica looked around them. "Maybe this place should be called Bent Corn rather than Bent Grass."

He couldn't stop the rolling of his eyes at her terrible joke, but then she started giggling. She fought valiantly to keep it silent, and mostly succeeded, but she couldn't seem to stop the huge grin that lit her face or the quiet laughter that shook her shoulders. As the sun hit her reddish-blond hair, her beauty as she crouched down to hide among the golden cornstalks overwhelmed him.

Growing up in the Amish community, where they didn't own any cameras or take any photographs since posing for a picture was considered prideful, he had trained himself to take mental images so he could remember specific moments in time.

Here in the field, he snapped a photo with his mind. This was a moment he would want to remember many times over in the future when this breathtaking woman had moved on from him and on with her life.

Veronica's joke had been bad, and truly not worthy of that much mirth. But laughter felt good, like a soothing balm to her soul, after their trials and tribulations the last couple of days. She had needed that release of anxiety and tension, and judging from the wide smile and relaxation of the lines on Matthew's face, he had needed that corny joke as well.

Reality wouldn't stay away, though.

"We should keep going," Matthew whispered. "To find you a telephone."

She could only nod, the truth of her situation crashing around her and flattening her like she had crushed the cornstalks in her hasty escape.

With another hand signal to stay put, Matthew rose to his feet slowly, peering through the stalks. A nanosecond later, he dropped to the ground again. His wide eyes and his nod in the direction of the house told her everything she needed to know.

Popov had not abandoned the chase.

Matthew held a finger to his lips to indicate complete silence. She nodded her agreement.

A few seconds ticked by, punctuated by a couple of footfalls on cornstalks. The hot musky odor of the ripening corn tickled her nostrils, and she swiped the back of her hand across her face to tame the itch of an impending sneeze. She couldn't let that happen. That loud *achoo* would get them discovered right quick. Veronica had lived in Indiana for many years, but she had never been this up close and personal to a cornfield. Under different circumstances, it could be fun to play hide-and-seek in the mature corn. This version of it, though, was not her idea of a game.

Only the sound of buzzing insects surrounded them. Her legs grew weak and began to tremble, but she didn't dare to sit down cross-legged lest she make noise and draw attention to their location. Sweat trickled down her back.

Footsteps sounded again. This time in retreat.

She looked to Matthew for what to do next, but he was staring straight ahead through the corn, leaning from side to side to see farther. His leg seemed to bother him, both physically and psychologically, from time to time. His vibe of frustration with his perceived lack of mobility came through loud and clear to Veronica. But it hadn't truly hindered him. She was safe, wasn't she? Still alive and in one piece, and on her way to a telephone.

Movement to her right caught her eye, and she swiveled her gaze to see what it was. Instantly, she pressed her lips together hard to squelch a scream. A large, black fuzzy spider skittered along a cornstalk. It stopped at eye level and seemed to turn to stare at her. Leaning back, she flailed out her arm to get Matthew's attention. Now, especially, she needed a hero.

"Matthew," she hissed, daring to whisper in the silence. Her hand made contact with his arm, and getting her fingers around his sleeve, she tugged at him. *"Matthew!"*

She refused to break eye contact with the spider. There was no telling where he might go when she wasn't watching. She felt Matthew turn toward her, his hand now grabbing her arm.

"What?"

Still not looking back at him, she pointed at the arachnid. "Spider!" she hissed.

"*Jah?* So?"

"Get it!" Why couldn't men understand the extreme importance of protecting their women from spiders?

"Do you know how many spiders are probably in this field right now?"

She could only shake her had. Without hesitation, Matthew flicked the spider. It flew through the air, landing several feet away.

Veronica inhaled deeply but didn't take her eyes off the spot where the thing had landed. She couldn't see it, but it was there somewhere, of that she had no doubt.

"*Ach*, are you alright?" Confusion tinged Matthew's low tone.

She finally turned to look at Matthew. Amusement crinkled the lines around his eyes. "Yes, I'm fine," she said quietly. She spun to survey the area. "Can we move on now?"

"Had enough of the outdoors?" His face crumpled as he fought hard not to break into a wide smile.

"At least of this cornfield." She rubbed her hands on her apron, even pulling the fabric in between her fingers to clean them off, but the stickiness she'd picked up from the corn stuck fast.

"I think they've retreated. For now." He stood and held out a hand to help her up. "Let's keep going, but step carefully. The stalks will crack when you step on them, and they can be very loud. Just in case, let's be as quiet as possible." He took a step forward, gingerly placing his foot in between the broken stalks.

They stepped through the flattened corn slowly and deliberately until they were back in the upright stalks. Feeling like she could breathe again, Veronica turned back to survey the area. It didn't seem as if anyone was following them.

As they continued on, Matthew held the stalks apart to step through then waited for Veronica to grab them before he went forward to the next row of stalks. It was a tedious process but seemed the only way.

But after one particularly thick row of corn, as Matthew turned to go forward a bit farther, he tripped over a root sticking up from the dirt. His arms flailed for something to grasp, and he fell forward. He landed first on his knees, releasing a loud "Oof!" Then his hands smacked the hard dirt.

Veronica hurried to get beside him, leaning over to try to see his face as he remained there on his hands and knees. She placed her hands on his back and shoulders as if she could lift him up. "Matthew, where did that root come from? I didn't see it, either. Are you okay? How can I help you?" She couldn't stop the onslaught of concerned questions as she tried to assess his situation.

Shrugging off her touch, he spun to sit down in the dirt. "*Jah*, I am fine. Physically, I think." He didn't make eye contact but murmured under his breath, "*Mein* pride is a bit wounded."

Choosing to ignore that comment, Veronica asked, "Can you get up?"

"*Ach*, I hope so." He pushed himself up with his hands, a grimace of pain tight across his eyes and lips. He stood still for a moment, his eyes closed, looking as if he was determining whether he had the endurance to continue to stand. "*Jah*, I'm *gut*," he said through gritted teeth.

"Shall I lead?"

"Jah. Denki."

But a few steps farther and it was abundantly clear that Matthew was not *gut*. His jaw clenched with every step of his handicapped leg.

An ache rose up in Veronica's throat as she whispered a prayer for Matthew to have the strength to continue. If she could alleviate the pain, she would in a thrice. Uncertain what to say, she just grabbed his hand. Hopefully, the physical touch would encourage him to do the best he could. "Should we rest for a bit? I haven't heard anything for a while, so I think we're safe here."

"Jah, perhaps." Veronica watched an internal struggle play out on his face in the ensuing silence, until he said, "You should *goh* on without me. Get to the telephone. Make the call. Arrange a meetup location. Then hide until the US Marshal gets there."

"What?" Surely, she hadn't heard him correctly.

"You need to get to safety. *Ach*, I'm slowing you down, so *goh* without me. You're strong and in good health. *Goh*." He rubbed the knee of his leg.

Was he out of his mind? *Ferhoodled?* Maybe the stress of being on the run was addling his brain? No way was she going to leave him there.

Absolutely not.

EIGHTEEN

A dull throbbing sensation ricocheted around Matthew's leg. He bent to massage his thigh muscle in what seemed like a vain attempt to heal himself.

Never in his life had he felt so ungraceful. So clumsy. So *embarrassed*.

Right in front of the woman he loved.

Jah, he loved her. He felt a grimace crease his face with the hopelessness of the entire situation.

On top of that, he couldn't get his brain to stop pinging with images he remembered from the fire that took the lives of his parents. Massive flames engulfing the structure, escaping through the windows to lick at the siding on the outside. Volunteer firefighters struggling with their massive hoses in a vain attempt to control the burn. Matthew on the outside, tears streaming, prayers lifting, heart breaking.

He couldn't save his parents. Why had he ever thought he could save Veronica? The irony struck him hard. The injury he had suffered in his failed attempt to save his parents hindered him now in a different rescue effort. And if he couldn't protect her, Veronica certainly wouldn't want any sort of lasting relationship with him.

Continuing to massage his knee and calf, he refused to

look up at her. How could he? She must be so very disappointed.

And then, a tender touch on his shoulder and a soft voice. "Matthew?"

He didn't respond. What could he say?

"I'm not leaving you." Veronica's gentle voice again.

Ach, now what? Her voice may be sweet and feminine and caring, but he knew her well enough by now to detect the underlying tone of determination. It was one of the character traits he loved about the *maedel*.

Still hunched over his leg, he began to pray fervently for healing, for strength, for courage to carry on. If he was going to continue with Veronica, he needed a special touch from *Gott*. A few whispers into his prayer, he heard Veronica's murmured prayer join his. Together, they sought the Lord until the final *amen*. He stood upright, an extra burst of energy surging through him, the ache in his leg significantly diminished.

Perhaps he really could be a strong protector. The leader of a family. But only with *Gott*'s help.

"*Denki* for praying for me." He turned to her, her vivid green eyes meeting his, filled with compassion and—did he dare to think it?—love. She ducked her head away from his gaze, her soft lips just inches from his. Should he kiss her?

As an invisible connection pulled him closer to her, cornstalks a couple of rows over cracked loudly in the hushed silence. Startled, he jerked his gaze to the direction of the noise, severing their connection.

Had Popov found them?

Veronica inched behind him, turning toward the sound of another stalk breaking as if someone was slowly walking toward them.

His heartbeat exploded as Matthew watched the cornstalks part a few feet away. A beautiful brown deer stepped out, staring at them with her large, startled eyes. He sagged as he released a breath he hadn't known he was holding. As the deer bounded away through the corn, Matthew realized the doe's presence had prevented what could have been a grave mistake.

Kissing Veronica.

"That felt like a close one." She stepped out from behind him, seemingly unaware of the possible double meaning of her words.

"*Jah.* And a *gut* reminder that we need to keep moving." Clenching his jaw, he stepped in front of her to lead in the right direction. He swiped his arm across his forehead to absorb the tacky perspiration that gathered there. Apparently, he had more courage to face down an angry man with a weapon than to reveal his heart to a beautiful woman.

It was every man's dilemma.

The sun shone high in the sky, and soon sweat trickled down Matthew's back. More than once in his peripheral vision, he saw Veronica, walking beside him but slightly behind, swipe at her brow. Humidity settled over them like a damp rag, blocking the brilliant blue of the sky and replacing it with the dull gray of water vapor in the air, much of it the remnant of the prior night's rainstorm. Being in the cornfield didn't help matters, either. It was the epicenter of humidity as the ripening corn cooled itself by releasing moisture into the air.

Veronica lagged behind with each step, until Matthew grabbed her hand to help her along. He watched carefully for roots and fallen stalks, and a half hour later, they emerged from the cornfield into a pasture surrounded by a homemade fence.

"Are we there?" Veronica stepped up beside him, a tired grin on her beautiful face.

"*Jah*, almost." He swiped his soggy sleeve across his forehead for the hundredth time. "This is the property of Zeke Beiler, my neighbor and friend. He's a *gut* man. You can use the phone he has for his buggy-building business to make your call, and for sure and for certain he'll lend us a buggy to get you to the meeting place you set up."

"Will he ask many questions?" Veronica pinched the skin at her throat as she scrutinized the distant buildings.

He completely understood her reluctance to meet someone new who didn't know their situation. "*Nee*. Zeke will be polite and respectful." Of course, the man would be naturally curious, but he wouldn't be pushy. That wasn't the Amish way. "We don't want to take too much time, anyway."

"Right. The longer we linger, the more chance Popov has to find us again." Veronica dropped his hand and hugged her arms around her middle. "Honestly, I don't know how much more running I can endure."

"*Jah*, it is almost over. I am sure." Matthew's spirit drooped within him. In fact, it was almost over, both their run for safety together as well as whatever relationship might have been forming. At least the almost kiss had been interrupted before he lost any more of his heart to this beautiful woman. He didn't know how much more heartbreak he could endure.

They skirted around the fence, a slight breeze whispering about them, lifting the stray strands of Veronica's hair off her forehead. As they walked, she straightened her *kapp*, redoing many of her bobby pins. Matthew didn't know any red-haired Amish *maedels*, and he prayed her strawberry-blond curls didn't attract undo attention from Zeke or anyone else they might encounter.

He spotted Zeke outside his barn and raised a hand in friendly greeting. He wasn't sure if the man could tell who it was at that distance, but surely he would recognize the Amish clothing and know it was a friend and not a foe.

As they drew closer, a curious look grew on the *mensch*'s face. Matthew had been a bachelor for many years, too old to attend singings where the young people usually found their mates, and had never been seen driving about with a female friend. So it made perfect sense that Zeke would be immensely curious about Matthew emerging from a cornfield, dirty and disheveled, in the company of a *maedel* who wore Amish clothing but up close and personal clearly was not Amish.

"*Hallo! Willkumme!*" Zeke called when they were still making their way around the field.

Veronica brushed her arm against Matthew's as they walked along the fence line. Did she wish she could hold his hand for support? If she didn't want to answer questions, it was best that she kept her distance.

"*Gut daag! Ach*, it is *gut* to see you, friend." Matthew grasped the *mensch*'s hand in a warm handshake.

"*Jah.*" Zeke's eyes flicked over Veronica, taking in her vibrant tresses—tucked as much as possible under the *kapp*—her soiled Amish dress, her gaze that refused to meet his. "Is everything alright?"

"We are alright." Matthew glanced at the woman beside him. That was more true than not. Clearly, life could be better. But they were safe and whole, and for that he would praise *Gott*. "But could we use your telephone?"

Zeke looked pointedly at Veronica without asking his

question aloud. Matthew only nodded. "*Jah*. You know where it is." He gestured toward the barn door.

An awkward silence rose between them as she peeled away from them and headed for the open door several feet away. When she disappeared inside, Zeke asked, "Is there anything else I can help you with?"

Now was his chance to unburden his soul, to tell this sort-of friend everything. But what would be the purpose in that? To feed the Amish gossip circles? *Nee*, he would keep it to himself for now. That is what Veronica would want. "*Actually*, we are in need of a horse and buggy, if you have one to spare. I need to get the *maedel*—" he didn't say her name as he nodded toward the barn door where Veronica had disappeared "—to a meeting place, and then I can bring it back."

"*Jah*, of course." Zeke smiled. "You have *kumme* to the right place. I would be out of business if I didn't have buggies."

The man led the way inside the barn. A half-dozen buggies in various states of construction and repair lined one wall. Veronica stood at a tall worktable just inside the door, the telephone to her ear.

"I will get one ready for you." Zeke slapped Matthew on the shoulder and headed toward the back of the barn.

"Denki." Gratitude for his friend's discretion in leaving them to their telephone call flooded him, and he made an instant determination that he would work on a better friendship with Zeke once this was all over.

Matthew joined Veronica at the worktable, her eyes wide as she watched him approach as she listened and murmured her agreement into the telephone receiver.

"Okay. I can do that. But where?" She turned to Matthew, putting the palm of her hand over the mouthpiece. "Where can I meet him?" she whispered to him.

He fought the urge to put a protective arm around Veronica's shoulders. "Are you sure you have the US Marshal? The *real* US Marshal?"

She pursed her lips at him but a smile played around the corners of her eyes. "Yes, I'm sure. I remembered the telephone number, and they have my file. They know everything about me, and I'm talking with the deputy marshal who will come get me. But he wants to know where we should meet."

"Someplace public, with a lot of people, for sure and for certain." He looked at the floor, visually tracing a crack in the floorboard, to help himself concentrate and not be distracted by Veronica's nearness. Even now, after all they had been through, he could smell the sweet apple aroma of her shampoo. "The public market. It'll be crowded with lots of tourists this time of day."

Veronica nodded her agreement and returned her concentration to her call. A few moments later, all was arranged and she replaced the receiver in the cradle.

Matthew didn't want to think that Zeke had been eavesdropping from elsewhere in his barn, but with uncanny timing, he emerged from the back recesses of the structure, driving a horse pulling an enclosed buggy. Matthew closed his eyes and uttered a quick prayer of thanks to *Gott*. Veronica had her meeting set up, they had a safe way to get there, and the market was just a few miles away.

She stepped up beside him. "Is this our ride?"

"*Jah, denki* to Zeke."

A couple of minutes later, Matthew pulled the buggy out of the barn, Veronica at his side, and waved to Zeke. As they rode down the lane and toward the road, he smiled at the beautiful woman next to him, taking another mental picture. He wanted to remember her as an Amish woman, with the pristine white *kapp* on her strawberry-blond locks and the apron tied around her slender waist. "We're on our way again. I think we're going to make it."

"I agree." She returned his smile. "Easy peasy lemon squeezy."

Matthew wouldn't have chosen that odd *Englisch* phrase. He would not have said it was easy. But if it made her face light up, he wouldn't disagree.

The breeze created by the buggy's motion cooled him, and after seeing no speeding *Englisch* cars, he turned the horse onto the two-lane asphalt road.

"How long will it be?" She settled back in the front seat, but Matthew noticed she still held herself in a stiff posture.

"It's five to ten miles away, so about a half hour. Will that work?"

"Yes. The deputy marshal will wait for me, whenever I arrive."

The clattering of a car engine sounded from behind them. Matthew's muscles tensed, and he could feel Veronica shrink into the seat. *Not again.* But the vehicle passed by them and continued on. "Not them," he murmured to her as he watched the bright red SUV drive down the road.

But as they crested a small hill, a dark-colored car approached from the opposite direction. It slowed as it passed them. A jolt of adrenaline shocked Matthew's system as he made eye contact with Nadia Popov, who sat in the passenger seat of the sedan. Veronica squealed beside him and clutched his arm.

Had they been seen? Had Popov recognized him?

A moment later, his question was answered when the dark sedan spun into a U-turn in the middle of the road. It accelerated until it jammed the rear bumper of the buggy. Matthew dug his feet into the floorboards as the impact tossed him forward. Veronica threw her arms out in front, and her palms hit the storm shield. Her scream ricocheted around the enclosed space.

Matthew clutched the reins, his brain frantically fighting for a solution.

Danger had found them again.

A second scream wailed throughout the buggy. Veronica clutched her raw and ragged throat. Was she the one screaming?

Cold washed over her as static buzzed so loudly in her ears that she could hear nothing else. She turned to Matthew. His mouth moved, as if he was trying to communicate with her, but she heard nothing except the clamoring in her head.

The buggy lurched forward again, and she kept herself from flying through the storm shield by planting her hands on the dashboard. Her wrists pained her fiercely, but she would deal with that later. As suddenly as it began, the static faded. Sounds became normal, although loud.

"Hold on," Matthew said.

Veronica looked over to see his grim expression that demonstrated an intense focus on the horse and the road. His arm muscles strained with his grip on the reins as he fought to keep the animal calm in the melee.

"What do we do?" She knew he would say so when he figured it out, but she couldn't stop herself from asking. Helplessness overwhelmed her.

"Working on it." He risked a glance at her then immediately returned his attention to the road.

Another jolt from behind threw her forward as the front

of the buggy bumped the horse's hindquarters. "How many times will they do that?" she exclaimed. Of course, no one could know, but she wasn't sure how much longer she could tolerate it.

Tossing his head, the horse turned back and forth, allowing Veronica to see the fiery indignation in his eye. No one should treat a horse like that, especially a good driving horse.

"The animal won't stand for it much longer." Matthew clutched the reins tighter. "Get ready."

"Ready for what?" What more would she have to endure simply because she had done the right thing all those years ago when she had told the truth about the atrocities she had witnessed? She finally had experienced just a hint of what a relationship could be. Her faith had been growing, she'd fallen in love and she was beginning to hope for a family and normalcy. How could that happen, though, as long as she was suffering at the hands of Nadia Popov and her henchman?

"A runaway horse. He's getting nervous." As they approached a hill with no other traffic in sight, Matthew loosened his grip on one of the reins.

Panic surged through Veronica. "God help us!" The words popped into her head and out her mouth without thinking.

"*Jah*, amen!"

The car slowed a bit behind them with the incline of the hill, but the man driving revved the engine and shot forward to slam the buggy again. The horse reared, both front hooves leaving the ground, a wild look in his eye.

Matthew let loose of one rein as the horse lunged forward, slowed by the upward tilt of the road. Veronica gripped the seat with one hand and the dashboard with the other, fully trusting that he knew what he was doing with the reins to keep the horse under control.

But as they crested the hill, a traffic jam awaited them on the other side. A white minivan loomed up in front of them, and Matthew hurried to pull back on the reins. Veronica sneaked a peek through the tiny back window to see the black sedan slow, suddenly keeping several feet of distance from the buggy's bumper. The last thing Popov and her driver would want was an accident right there with eyewitnesses. Their attack was going to have to wait until they both reached the other side of the traffic.

With trembling hands, Veronica turned back to the front, leaning to the right and left trying to see what was holding them up. Several vehicles lined up in front of them along with a few buggies on the side of the road. Farther ahead, a couple of police cars with lights flashing had pulled over a semitruck and trailer. Traffic had been reduced to one lane. Chaos reigned as drivers fought to get their turn to go around the blockage.

"Praise *Gott* for answering our prayers." Matthew relaxed back into the seat. "I think we are okay for now, at least as long as we're in this traffic. I'll figure something out before we get to the other side."

He was right, of course, but her mind filled with a jumbled, confused mess of words. As she struggled with a response, tears sprang out in sudden, uncontainable sobs. She had never felt so out of control, and she had no idea how to regain it.

A startled look flitted across Matthew's face. Mopping her face with the hem of her apron, she hiccuped the first cohesive thought that came into her mind. "Why is this happening to me?"

Putting both reins in one hand, Matthew covered her hand on the seat with his and slowly released a breath.

She continued between hiccups before he could respond. "Popov is free. If she's caught, she goes back to prison on the original crime. So there's nothing more I can do to hurt her. Why doesn't she just run away? Go someplace where she won't be found? Why try to kill me?"

Matthew squeezed her hand and checked all around, but they remained stuck in the line of traffic. "We cannot know what's in her mind. That is only for *Gott* to know. But I've read a lot of crime thrillers, and the motive of the villain is usually revenge. In some odd way, the villain usually thinks he'll feel better if the person he believes caused all of his trouble is dead."

"That doesn't make much sense. They'd still be in the same trouble if I was dead. In fact, as soon as they're caught, she's in more trouble because she broke out of prison. Killing me isn't going to make that go away."

"*Jah*, you are right. And revenge is not the Amish way because it's not *Gott*'s way. True repentance is the only cure that will solve her problems and heal her." They had inched closer to the traffic stop, and Matthew leaned in front of Veronica to peer out her window. "I have a plan to get you to the market, but we're going to have to continue on foot."

"Whatever it takes." They were so close to safety, and Matthew had done so much for her. She couldn't wimp out now.

He turned to her with a grim look filled with such determination that extra energy and enthusiasm burst through her. "To get around the police vehicles and the semi," he said and nodded in that direction, "I'm going to have to pull into the middle of the road with the rest of the traffic. Once we pass them, I'll pull back over to the shoulder. For a few seconds, this right side of the buggy where you're sitting will be hidden from view by the cab of the semi. We'll sneak out that side and head into the woods. I know a footpath that'll get us to the market. It's well-known to the Amish, but it's not obvious to someone who doesn't know it's there."

A fluttering coursed through her at the idea of a successful getaway. "You think it'll work?"

"*Jah*, it's our best option."

"What about the horse? How will he get home if we leave him?"

"He will be fine in the grass on the side of the road until I can return for him. Or if someone who knows Zeke finds him, they'll bring him home." He pressed her hand. "We have to get you to safety, Veronica. That's the priority."

She nodded. What else could she do? There was no other alternative. They were out of options.

They passed the police cars and the semitruck, the dark sedan keeping a sizable distance between them but still close enough that the man could surely see everything.

"We're almost there," Matthew said as he urged her to scoot to the edge of the seat. He inched closer as well.

At the massive white hood of the truck, he pulled on the reins, and the horse promptly swerved them onto the shoulder. Veronica's muscles tensed in anticipation. Matthew led the animal into the grass, and with a whispered "*Go!*" and a nudge on her shoulder, she leaped out of the buggy, swinging down as she grasped the metal handrail and landed on both feet in the grass.

A moment later, Matthew stood beside her, the buggy stopped on the edge of the shoulder, the horse lowering his head to the grass. He grabbed her hand and led her into the woods. "It won't be long now," he murmured with an encouraging squeeze of her hand. "If they stop the car and follow us, they'll only draw attention to themselves. That wouldn't be wise with that police officer right there."

Several feet into the brush, they ducked behind a large tree and looked back toward the road just in time to see the dark sedan pass slowly, the Popov woman examining the woods with a scowl on her face. Sunlight glinted off the barrel of the gun she held, resting against the bottom edge of the window.

Veronica jerked back behind the tree, yanking Matthew with her. The bark exploded, bits of wood flying around them. Her stomach clenched within her as she forced herself to stand like a statue. Holding her breath, she refused to be seen, let alone caught, after all this time and effort running. Several seconds passed before Matthew peeked around the tree trunk again. "They're gone," he breathed.

A sigh escaped as she collapsed against the tree, the rough bark pressing into her skin. "So we're safe?"

"*Jah.* For now." He stepped away, still holding her hand before the path narrowed. "Let's get you to the market."

Veronica followed in silence for several minutes, her heartbeat gradually slowing to a normal rate as she watched the sunlight filter through the treetops. Was this her last walk with this man she had come to know and love? Would she ever see him again? Her free hand rose involuntarily to press against her chest as if that would stop the ache that was beginning to rise within her. She had to say something. The end was near, and she would regret it for the rest of her days if she didn't speak up and at least give him a chance to respond. If he didn't want her, an *Englischer* who had brought only danger to his life, then at least she would know she had tried.

"Matthew?" Her voice quivered, despite her best effort to keep it neutral.

"Jah?" He continued walking but slowed slightly.

Her brain froze. How to start? "Um, are we being fol-lowed?" It was the best she could stutter out.

He turned to check behind. *"Nee,* we are alone." His eyes widened when they met hers. *"Ach,* what is it? We are on the move, and I believe we'll be at the market soon."

A tear escaped and coursed down her cheek. She swiped it away. "I know. I just… I was wondering…will I ever see you again?" This wasn't how she had wanted to ask, but the thought of all that aloneness again, back in WITSEC, made her heart sink.

Matthew grasped her arms in his warm hands, a smile growing across his handsome face. "Do you want to see me again?"

Veronica ducked her head, suddenly feeling like she'd said too much. But she couldn't deny it now. *"Jah.* I do."

"Jah, me, too." He pulled her closer. "I've fallen in love with you, and I dread losing you back into witness pro-tection. They'll move you somewhere and give you a new name, and I'll never see you again."

"Maybe I could join an Amish protection program?" That sounded quite presumptuous to her own ears, but it was out of her mouth before she could think through it.

Before she could take it back or explain herself, he low-ered his lips to hers, and the trees and the sunshine and the awkwardness faded away in the warmth of his kiss.

NINETEEN

So this was what perfect bliss was like.

Even though he wanted the kiss to continue forever, Matthew pulled away, the empty void of separation seeping in between them.

"*Mein liebchen*, I will create an Amish protection program specifically for you, if you wish." His heart pounded within him. Could this really be happening? To him? He had waited and wondered and prayed for so many years that *Gott* might send him someone to love. And now, was she here in his arms?

Or *was* she? The top of her head came up to his chin, and he inhaled deeply of the apple scent of her reddish-blond hair. *Jah*, she was beautiful and fun and warm and caring. But she was also an *Englischer*. He was baptized into the Amish church. If he left, he would be shunned, never to see or talk to his *schwester*, his *aendi* and *oncle*, his friends again. He would not be allowed back, or if he did try to visit, they could turn their backs on him or make him eat at a separate table. His faith in *Gott* and the Amish lifestyle would not allow him to leave. As much as he loved Veronica, he could think of no worse fate than to lose his relationship with *Gott*.

But would she join the Amish church? Was that what she had intended with her words?

Veronica was a survivor. She had had to be. In her world, that meant not getting too close to people. Keeping them at arm's length. Maintaining her new secret identity in WIT-SEC meant not only could she not risk being discovered, but she also couldn't risk putting anyone, especially someone she cared about, in harm's way simply due to them having knowledge of her situation. And that's exactly what she'd been doing with him. Holding him at a distance. Whether or not it was pure instinct after all these years didn't matter. It was what it was and would be difficult, nearly *impossible*, to overcome.

When she didn't reply, he pulled back and asked, "Ready to keep going?" He tried to force his heart to separate from her, to turn away from her just as he made his body turn away, to continue through the woods. But his heart rebelled, pounding against his chest as if trying to break free from the hurt.

Letting loose of her hand, he continued down the path as it gradually narrowed to a width only wide enough for single file. The trees grew thick, and Matthew couldn't see through them to the end of the path.

"Matthew?" Her quiet voice jolted his spirit. "How does someone become Amish?"

He stumbled over a rock in the path, coming down on his disabled leg, and she reached to help him up. It was a harsh reminder that he was not, and never could be, good enough for her. "You are born into it. The Amish don't evangelize and try to bring new people in."

"But what if someone wanted to become Amish who wasn't born into an Amish family? Is that possible?"

"*Jah*, I suppose." What was she getting at? "But it would be difficult."

"How so?"

"This new convert would have to be ready to leave the modern world behind. As you've seen, we live without electricity or cars or cell phones. Do you know any *Englischer* who would be willing to give up their phone?" He could see the helpfulness of such a device, but was immensely glad he didn't have the opportunity to become hooked.

"I would love to get rid of that device." Her voice was so quiet he doubted that he had heard her right. Was she asking for herself? His palms were slick with nervous perspiration.

"We dress differently. Sometimes people look at us like we're odd."

"I've been wearing the Amish dress for a few days now. I like it. It feels feminine. And it reduces decision fatigue since I don't have to figure out what I'm going to wear every day." Her voice grew in strength. "What else?"

Was she serious? It seemed she was talking about herself. He let himself dream it was true for just a moment before levying the most important requirement. "Faith in Jesus Christ as your Lord and Savior. That's the number-one commitment in the Amish church and community." He had had his struggles over the years, especially the time right after his parents had been killed in the fire. But he had never seriously contemplated leaving his faith. Veronica didn't have that foundation, at least not for the majority of her life. That influence had died with her parents.

Her answer shook him to his core, hope bursting and blossoming within him like the bluebells and wild geraniums and tiger lilies that surrounded them. "I can make that commitment. I do believe."

He spun back to her, reaching for both of her hands with his. "Truly, *jah*?"

She nodded, moisture glistening around her eyes.

"So…are these questions about you? About *you* joining the Amish church?"

She nodded, a whispered *yes* floating between them.

"What about…?" He lowered his head, suddenly unable to make eye contact, and kicked at a rock in the path. "Would I still be able to see you? Could we be friends?" He didn't have the confidence to ask for more than that.

Without a word, she lifted his chin, looked him in the eye and kissed him on the lips. "Does that answer your question?"

"*Jah*," he murmured as he ran his fingertips down her cheek. He wanted to pinch himself but he couldn't pull his hands away from holding her. A bird trilled loudly nearby, jerking him out of his reverie. Reality jolted him awake. The Amish life was so very different from the *Englisch* life with so many issues to think through. Could she truly do it?

He turned back to continue leading her to the market. As much as he might want it, they couldn't stay in the woods, in that moment, forever. "What about your business of writing cookbooks and your blog?"

"Couldn't I keep doing that? It's my job, and I'd need to make money to support myself. It's my bread and butter, if you'll pardon a bad joke. Plus, I really like it."

Matthew could see her point. "*Jah*, it's like an Amish family with a woodworking business or a dairy farm or a quilt shop."

"Exactly."

"Well, for business purposes, the bishop would probably allow you to keep your computer and internet connection.

We have an Amish newspaper that has computers and a social-media profile."

As they walked, she tapped her fingers against his back in her excitement. "I would need an office. Since the Amish like barns, maybe I could have a she-shed."

"*Jah*, whatever that is." He smiled at her enthusiasm. Now, if only *Gott* would heal his leg, he could be enough for her. "As much as I like your plans, we need to keep moving. The longer we linger, the more chance that woman has to find us. All this talk is for naught if you are captured or killed." Matthew could not bear that, especially not now, not after those kisses and the talk of Veronica joining the Amish.

The trees began to thin with more sunlight streaming in as he spied the edge of the woods up ahead. A vast field would be the first expanse for them to cross, and the market would be on the other side. Safety and security were within reach, and he pushed himself to pick up the pace.

"Is that it?" Veronica double-stepped to get up beside him as the path widened.

"*Jah*. Hopefully, safety is up ahead." Matthew grabbed her hand as they took the last few steps out of the trees.

A large two-story structure sat on the other side of the field with cars in a parking lot and people coming and going. An unmarked beige SUV stood at the edge closest to the field. A man, tiny at that distance, stood beside it, looking in their direction.

"Is that the deputy marshal?" Veronica raised her hand to wave.

"*Nee.*" Matthew pulled her palm down before she could signal him. "Don't draw any attention to us. I am eager for an end to this running as well, but we don't want to cause any more trouble now that we're so close."

"Yeah, that makes sense." With her half-raised hand, she felt the security of her *kapp*. "But is that him?"

"I believe so." He turned to smile at her and squeezed her fingers. "Let's go find out."

Veronica bounced on her toes a couple of times before following him, swinging his arm in her anticipation. He paused, surveying the edge of the woods to the left and to the right and then throughout the field. Other than a slight murmur from the activity at the market, only noises from the woods reached him. The wind ruffled the leaves in the trees, and small animals scurried about. Popov, her thug and the dark sedan were nowhere to be seen.

Releasing a large breath slowly and still gripping Veronica's hand, he continued on the path that led through the middle of the field. With each step, his heart grew lighter, but he maintained his surveillance of the surrounding area. He could not tolerate any sort of misstep now that they were so close to being out of harm's way.

As they crossed through the grass, the Deputy US Marshal's form grew larger and more lifelike. Matthew inhaled deeply and blew out a breath slowly. It seemed that after all the danger, they were going to make it.

But halfway through the field, Veronica leaned down to swat away a mosquito on her ankle. Matthew turned in a 360-degree circle to survey their surroundings.

There, at the edge of the woods, right where they had emerged, stood Nadia Popov. A glint of sunlight reflected off metal.

With a steady hand, she raised a gun.

It was pointed directly at them.

"Help! Over here!"

Startled by Matthew's yell, Veronica's fingers tightened on her shoelace as her heart beat out a fierce staccato rhythm. Eye level with the tall shoots of foxtail grass, she watched the deputy draw his weapon and point it in their direction.

Nausea struck her with full force. Another imposter? Had it all been a set up to get her to come in so Popov could finally kill her?

"Veronica." Matthew's voice finally reached her through the whooshing sound in her ears. "We need to move. Now."

She stood quickly, Matthew grasping her elbow. He took a few steps forward, pulling her, but her feet were rooted to the spot. She wasn't going to move closer to the man who had his gun pointed at her. "He's not a real deputy marshal. It's another trick. We need to go the other way."

Breaking free of his hold, she spun back to the woods. Best to escape the way they came. Matthew knew the path and the woods. He could lead her so she could evade capture. *Again.*

But at the edge of the woods, right in the path's opening, stood Nadia Popov. Her hands held the weapon steady. The weapon that pointed directly at her heart.

Veronica's breathing grew faster until she saw block spots in her vision, her hands fisted at her sides.

The man on the other side of the field must be the guy she had seen with Popov. Her thug.

And Veronica was caught in the middle. In between two evil people who wanted her dead.

A scream ripped from her throat. Her muscles rigid, she could only stare at the woman. Her body couldn't even remember to blink.

Tearing her gaze from Popov, she backed away with quick jerky steps, stumbling over the uneven ground. She bumped into Matthew.

"*Nee*, not that way." His hand on her arms, he turned her one-hundred and eighty degrees, back toward the market.

"He's with her," she hissed, finally finding her voice, "and we're in the middle. We're caught." She swallowed hard. "Or dead."

"*Ach*, he's the deputy marshal." Matthew paused as if unsure. "Isn't he? He's pointing his gun at Popov."

"Is he?" They were frozen, unable to know what to do or which way to go.

An explosion of gunfire ripped through the air behind them. A bullet whizzed past, inches from Veronica's shoulder. Popov had shot at her.

Matthew spun on his strong leg to get behind her, in between Veronica and the woman shooting.

But should they go forward? What about the man pointing the gun at them?

Before she could take a single step, the man at the edge of the field yelled as she stared straight at them. *"Get down!"*

From behind, both of his hands on her shoulders, Matthew pushed Veronica to the ground. She fell face-first into the dirt, Matthew going down with her, covering her with his body.

Another shot exploded, this time from the side of the field where the deputy marshal stood. Then another and another. Veronica kept her face in the dirt as the bullets whizzed above her head.

Then silence. A breeze ruffled the grass. A bee buzzed by.

Finally, Matthew lifted himself just enough to peer through the blades of grass. "He shot her. She's down."

A moment later, black men's shoes appeared in the grass beside them. Veronica lifted her head and shoulders to see a man in body armor labeled US Marshal standing over them.

Matthew stood and then held out a hand to help her up. "Are you alright, *mein liebchen*?" Worry creased the lines about his eyes.

"*Jah*," she answered in her best Pennsylvania German accent. She turned to see another couple of men in matching vests with Nadia Popov. One handcuffed her as another applied a tourniquet above her knee where her pants were soaked with blood.

"Are you both okay?" The deputy marshal visually examined them up and down, pausing at Matthew's leg as he bent to brush dirt and grass off his broadfall trousers.

Matthew looked at Veronica. She nodded. "*Jah*, we're fine," he answered.

"And you are Veronica Williams?" The man pierced her with his intense look, a reassurance that he took his job and her safety seriously.

"Yes." She turned to Matthew. "This is Matthew Yoder. He's been keeping me safe these past couple of days."

The deputy marshal shook Matthew's hand. "I'd say that's a job well done."

A smile grew across his face as Veronica thought she felt him release a breath. Was he thinking of his parents and the fire and his disability? She uttered a silent prayer that this would be the boost of confidence he needed.

"*Denki.*" Matthew nodded. "Thank you."

"Now, let's get you two to safety. We're still hunting for Popov's cohort."

At the edge of the field, the deputy marshal put them in the back of his SUV. Another officer sat in the front passenger seat, his attention keeping a vigil on all that happened outside.

Within the next few minutes, the man who had been with Popov pulled into the market parking lot in the dark sedan. He swung around to park, scanning the field as if looking for someone. Instantly, more marshals dressed in plain clothes who apparently had been blending into the crowd or sitting in other vehicles emerged to surround the car, weapons drawn. Soon, the man stood in handcuffs, pressed against the sedan, the crowd of tourists held back at a safe distance, listening as a US Marshal read him his Miranda rights.

Still with some trepidation, Veronica relaxed into the comfortable leather seat. She took a long drink from a water bottle, letting the coolness trickle down her throat and soothe her spirit.

As they watched the US Marshal's SUV pull out of the parking lot with Popov and her henchman in custody, Matthew gently took her hand and laced his fingers through hers. "I think it's over, *mein liebchen.*"

"Jah." She laid her head against his shoulder and closed her eyes, breathing deeply of the soothing scent of woods and leather. "It's over."

EPILOGUE

Veronica raised the window, lifted her face to the sunshine and inhaled deeply. Although the clematis still wasn't blooming well, the trellis she and Matthew had used to escape had been repaired and stood tall again. A shudder shook her, but she pushed it away. There was no more need for fear or worry. It had been helpful when she needed it, but the witness protection program was now a thing of the past.

She was free.

Not only was she free of WITSEC and constant surveillance and the threat of danger, but she was also free indeed because the Son had set her free. She was still a work in process, and some days it seemed that the cogs were moving slowly. After several intense sessions of learning and study and prayers with the bishop, Veronica had been baptized into the Amish church.

It would take a while to get used to it all. To freedom and safety. She still wanted to look over her shoulder and keep her go bag prepped and ready. But slowly, she was healing, and that was a wonderful and peaceful feeling.

With one more deep breath of the fresh autumn air, she returned to the second-floor apartment's bathroom. With a few months of growth, her strawberry-blond hair had become quite long, although it was still an oddity among the

Amish. Now, she quickly twisted it up into a bun, secured it with several bobby pins and fastened on her starched white *kapp*.

Matthew had been gracious enough to let her live in the apartment above his bookstore. She supposed she would get her own place eventually. But for now, she needed time to figure out what her life would look like going forward. She stopped at the kitchenette and poured a cup of *kaffee* then headed down to the store.

With the store still closed in the early morning hours, she said *gut morge* to Matthew, who had already arrived from the *haus* he shared with Esther and was stocking new Bibles on the shelf. In the office, she settled into the second desk he had squeezed into the small space and opened her laptop. The church bishop had encouraged her to continue writing her cookbooks and her blog and had, in fact, helped Matthew find this desk that was now her workspace. In just a couple of months, her first Amish cookbook would hit the shelves.

Before she opened her manuscript to begin for the day, she opened the desk drawer where she kept the photo of ten-year-old Veronica with her *schwesters*. They had all been so happy then. Would she ever see them again? Would they share that joy some day? She said a prayer for their well-being as well as for their reunion someday and then replaced the picture in the drawer.

"Veronica?"

She turned to see Matthew in the doorway. An odd look covered his face, but he adjusted it to a smile as soon as she spun in her chair. *"Jah?"*

His smile grew at her use of the Amish word. "Could you *kumme* here for a moment?"

She stood and followed him to the section of Bibles and

devotional books. He picked up one of the new Bibles and opened it. "Is there a problem with the inventory?" Why had he called her here? She didn't typically help much with the stock. She had been happy to rearrange some of the sections and decorate a bit to make the store more inviting, even making suggestions for what he could carry to appeal more to *Englisch* customers. But ordering was his department.

"*Nee.* I think all is well." He handed her the Bible, pointing out a particular passage.

Was this more Bible study? She had read the entire Book through once and was now going back to study more in-depth. Did he have more to add? She took the Bible and followed his finger to the verse in Genesis. "'And the Lord God said, It is not good that the man should be alone—I will make him an help meet for him.'" She looked up at him, feeling her eyebrows pull together as she tried to figure his purpose.

Matthew cleared his throat. "It is not *gut* that a *mensch* should be alone."

Silence passed between them as he looked at the books on the shelf and then on the floor.

What was his problem?

"*Jah*, that is what the Scripture says." Should she just ask him outright what his point was?

"I do not want to be alone anymore." His face flushed as he met her gaze. "I want to be married."

Veronica's breath caught as a hand fluttered involuntarily to her throat. What exactly did that mean? She opened her mouth but only a stuttering came out.

"I love you, *mein liebchen*. Will you marry me?"

Her heart bursting, she could only nod as he leaned in to kiss her.

The scent of books hung strong around them with a hint of the *kaffee* she had left in the office. Early morning sunshine streamed in the large windows at either end of the bookstore, displaying dancing dust motes in the slanting rays. As Matthew leaned in to kiss her again, she couldn't imagine a better moment.

From now on, she would hide in plain sight.

* * * * *

Dear Reader,

Sometimes it can be difficult to discover who God made us to be. Sure, we have legal documentation such as a driver's license and a social security card, but those things do not determine our core. The Lord, the One who knit us together in the womb, can reveal to us who He wants us to be if we seek Him.

Veronica Williams, with her years in the witness protection program, was unaware that her true identity was found in Jesus Christ and not in her forms of identification. Matthew Yoder, avoiding who he was, was hiding behind his handicapped leg, believing he was inferior and unwanted. Yet the Lord, in His perfect timing, brought them together to discover not only who they were individually, but also who they were together. He will show us who we are if we just ask.

May the Lord richly bless you,
Meghan Carver

Get up to 4 Free Books!

We'll send you 2 free books from each series you try PLUS a free Mystery Gift.

FREE Value Over **$25**

Both the **Love Inspired®** and **Love Inspired® Suspense** series feature compelling novels filled with inspirational romance, faith, forgiveness and hope.

YES! Please send me 2 FREE novels from the Love Inspired or Love Inspired Suspense series and my FREE gift (gift is worth about $10 retail). After receiving them, if I don't wish to receive any more books, I can return the shipping statement marked "cancel." If I don't cancel, I will receive 6 brand-new Love Inspired Larger-Print books or Love Inspired Suspense Larger-Print books every month and be billed just $7.19 each in the U.S. or $7.99 each in Canada. That is a savings of 20% off the cover price. It's quite a bargain! Shipping and handling is just 50¢ per book in the U.S. and $1.25 per book in Canada.* I understand that accepting the 2 free books and gift places me under no obligation to buy anything. I can always return a shipment and cancel at any time by calling the number below. The free books and gift are mine to keep no matter what I decide.

Choose one: ☐ **Love Inspired Larger-Print**
(122/322 BPA G36Y)

☐ **Love Inspired Suspense Larger-Print**
(107/307 BPA G36Y)

☐ **Or Try Both!**
(122/322 & 107/307 BPA G36Z)

Name (please print)

Address

Apt. #

City

State/Province

Zip/Postal Code

Email: Please check this box ☐ if you would like to receive newsletters and promotional emails from Harlequin Enterprises ULC and its affiliates. You can unsubscribe anytime.

Mail to the **Harlequin Reader Service:**
IN U.S.A.: P.O. Box 1341, Buffalo, NY 14240-8531
IN CANADA: P.O. Box 603, Fort Erie, Ontario L2A 5X3

Want to explore our other series or interested in ebooks? Visit **www.ReaderService.com** or call 1-800-873-8635.

---

*Terms and prices subject to change without notice. Prices do not include sales taxes, which will be charged (if applicable) based on your state or country of residence. Canadian residents will be charged applicable taxes. Offer not valid in Quebec. This offer is limited to one order per household. Books received may not be as shown. Not valid for current subscribers to the Love Inspired or Love Inspired Suspense series. All orders subject to approval. Credit or debit balances in a customer's account(s) may be offset by any other outstanding balance owed by or to the customer. Please allow 4 to 6 weeks for delivery. Offer available while quantities last.

LIRLIS25